Love,
Hollywood
Style

How NOT to Spend
Your Senior Year
BY CAMERON DOKEY

Royally Jacked
BY NIKI BURNHAM

Ripped at the Seams
BY NANCY KRULIK

Spin Control
BY NIKI BURNHAM

Cupidity
BY CAROLINE GOODE

South Beach Sizzle
BY SUZANNE WEYN AND
DIANA GONZALEZ

She's Got the Beat
BY NANCY KRULIK

30 Guys in 30 Days
BY MICOL OSTOW

Animal Attraction
BY JAMIE PONTI

A Novel Idea
BY AIMEE FRIEDMAN

Scary Beautiful
BY NIKI BURNHAM

Getting to Third Date
BY KELLY McCLYMER

Dancing Queen
BY ERIN DOWNING

Major Crush
BY JENNIFER ECHOLS

Do-Over
BY NIKI BURNHAM

Love Undercover
BY JO EDWARDS

Prom Crashers
BY ERIN DOWNING

Gettin' Lucky
BY MICOL OSTOW

The Boys Next Door
BY JENNIFER ECHOLS

In the Stars
BY STACIA DEUTSCH AND
RHODY COHON

Crush du Jour
BY MICOL OSTOW

The Secret Life
of a Teenage Siren
BY WENDY TOLIVER

Available from Simon Pulse

Love, Hollywood Style

P.J. RUDITIS

Simon Pulse
New York London Toronto Sydney

This book is a work of fiction. Any references to historical events, real people, or real locales are used fictitiously. Other names, characters, places, and incidents are the product of the author's imagination, and any resemblance to actual events or locales or persons, living or dead, is entirely coincidental.

SIMON PULSE
An imprint of Simon & Schuster Children's Publishing Division
1230 Avenue of the Americas, New York, NY 10020
Copyright © 2008 by Paul Ruditis
All rights reserved, including the right of reproduction in whole or in part in any form.
SIMON PULSE and colophon are registered trademarks of Simon & Schuster, Inc.
Designed by Ann Zeak
The text of this book was set in Garamond 3.
Manufactured in the United States of America
First Simon Pulse edition January 2008
10 9 8 7 6 5 4 3 2 1
Library of Congress Control Number 2007931731
ISBN-13: 978-1-4169-5138-4
ISBN-10: 1-4169-5138-5

To all my friends
from the page days

One

"I'm not supposed to tell you this." I spoke in a voice slightly above a whisper, forcing more than a dozen bodies to lean forward so they could hear me. "But this is the exact spot where Christy Caldwell is sitting in the opening shot of her upcoming film, *Table for Two*. You know, the scene they show in all the commercials, where she's eating alone at a fancy restaurant and she thinks everyone is laughing at her."

I waited as the tourists processed this information, scanning them for those tell-tale signs of confusion—a tilted head or a furrowed brow. I found one on the face of a dad from Wichita. His mismatched pale legs and sunburned face was something we often saw in midsummer at Sovereign Studios. It's the sign of someone who never gets out of the office and doesn't wear shorts or know the proper method of applying suntan lotion.

"But, Tracy," he said, double-checking with my name tag to confirm he got my name right. "You said this was a movie theater."

I did my best to suppress a smile as we stood in the lobby of the Sovereign Theater. It was such a help when the tourists unknowingly went along with the script I laid out in my mind. "And that, my friends, is what we call movie magic." Now they all broke into smiles as if that line explained everything. "All the director does is show an establishing shot of the outside of a real restaurant, and then the inside can be anywhere she wants. Throw in some tables and chairs, a waiter or two, and what used to be the lobby of a movie theater becomes an elegant restaurant. Last week this same lobby was used as a church in a music video."

Several people nodded their heads in awe while they tried to picture the theater lobby as a church. I could tell they were having trouble seeing it. The Sovereign

Theater lobby doesn't have a concession stand or anything of the tackiness of a public theater, but it certainly doesn't have the stained glass windows and wooden pews of the church I grew up in.

It probably would have been easier for the tourists to imagine if a half dozen people weren't in the process of hanging a huge banner in the middle of the lobby of Christy Caldwell dressed in a slinky black dress. The premiere of her new film, *Table for Two*, was scheduled in a few hours. Everyone was just at the point of scrambling to get the theater ready for the celebrities, studio big-wigs, and paparazzi who would be showing up later. Fearing that we were about to be kicked out for being in the way, I led my tour out of the theater lobby to continue the Sovereign Studios tour.

It was my second summer as a page at Sovereign Studios, so I was pretty good at knowing when it was time to move the tour along before I got yelled at for interfering with the working studio. Besides, I was also scheduled to work the premiere later, so I didn't want anyone angry with me who could make my life miserable. Pages are at the bottom of just about every food chain on the lot, so it's always good to make sure you don't give anyone a reason to report you to the boss.

By the way, "page" is the formal name for tour guides. Pages also fill in around the lot doing different odds and ends where needed, like working a movie premiere or helping catalog dusty, old archive boxes that have been stored under a soundstage for a few decades. The job isn't exactly all that glamorous.

During the school year, the pages are all college graduates, but the page staff is supplemented by high school and college students for the summer travel season. Even though they only make slightly above minimum wage—and sometimes have to give walking tours in hundred-degree heat—being at Sovereign Studios looks pretty good on the resume. Having graduated high school a month earlier, I'd been thinking a lot about my résumé that summer. And I still had four years of college to get through before I even started looking for a real job.

"It looks like they've finished laying the red carpet," I said, once we were back outside the theater. I looked over to one of the workmen. He knew what I was thinking as he waved me along. I gave him a thankful smile and nod as I turned to my tour group. "Anyone want to walk it?"

"You mean we're allowed?" asked a girl who was clearly younger than the twelve-year-old age limit for the tour.

"Go right ahead," I said with a flourish of my arm as I escorted my tour group onto the red carpet.

The tourists beamed as they walked down the carpet. Even though there was no one around but workmen—and we were walking away from the theater instead of into it—I can't imagine that any of them had ever walked a real Hollywood red carpet before. Then again, neither had I, so I have to admit I was also a little thrilled by the experience. And I was totally caught off guard when the flashbulbs started going off.

I squelched my momentary panic as I scanned my group for cameras. Tourists are only allowed to take pictures at three studio-approved photo spots. The studio is very strict about that and I clearly briefed my tour group before we started. I could get in a lot of trouble if any pictures of the setup for the premiere of *Table for Two* showed up on TMZ.com.

My panic was unwarranted, though. Nobody had a camera out. Everyone was simply walking along, enjoying the sights, hardly noticing the flashing lights that seemed to be coming from above.

I looked up to see my friend Dex on a scaffold hanging lights for the premiere. Dex was a part-time lighting apprentice and full-time aspiring actor who, along with his sister, Liz, I'd been friends with since kindergarten. In fact, his parents were the ones who got me the job at Sovereign Studios the summer before senior year.

Dex was flipping some of the lights on and off to imitate the flashes of the paparazzi. Leave it to Dex to come up with a perfect way to make my tour all the more memorable. I let out a relieved sigh and raised my arm in his direction.

"Everyone wave to the paparazzi," I said as the tourists turned toward the flashing lights and struck their best poses. The little girl even did the patented Paris Hilton "turn and glance over the shoulder" move that the celebutante made famous. It was a little disturbing to see a girl who couldn't be more than eight imitating Paris, but I'd seen worse in Hollywood.

In fact, I was seeing worse at that moment.

A mail cart with a distinctive pirate flag hanging on one side was driving in our direction. It was the one mail cart—or, more specifically, the one mail cart *driver*— that I had hoped I could avoid running into during my tour . . . or *ever*.

I had a brief moment of panic as we continued down the carpet. Considering the distance, we were going to come to the end at the same time the cart passed by. I thought about stopping the tour to point something—anything—out to them, but I didn't want to call any attention to myself, lest the driver see me. Instead, I slid in behind the rather tall, partially sunburned tourist from Wichita and hoped for the best while scrunching down as much as I could, trying to make myself invisible.

Dex shot me an odd look from his light tower, but didn't yell out to ask me what I was doing. I couldn't blame him for being confused. I didn't usually guide my tours hunched over and frog-walking. But if he had realized what was coming down the paseo, he would have understood. He had known me long enough to know about my history with guys and how sometimes it was easier to avoid them than to deal with them.

My group continued down the carpet while I silently prayed that the driver of the mail cart wouldn't see me. I also hoped that the tourists didn't notice I'd suddenly become very quiet and was effectively hiding in the middle of them. When the young Paris Hilton wannabe looked up at me to ask a question, I silently shook my head. Thankfully, she took the message and asked her mom instead.

"Mom, why is Tracy hiding behind Dad?" she called out, loudly, to her mom who was somewhere in front of us.

Thanks, kid, I thought as the group reached the end of the carpet.

I peeked out from behind Little Paris's dad and saw the pirate flag flapping in the breeze as the mail cart passed without slowing. Once I was sure the driver was out of earshot, I continued my tour. "And now when you get home you can tell all your friends you walked the same red carpet as Christy Caldwell," I said. "You don't have to say anything about walking it five hours *before* her, though."

Every single tourist got that familiar

gleam in his or her eye. They all tend to get that same look when I give them interesting exaggerations for when they get back home. I'm sure more than a couple of them were already working on lies to make it sound like they were special guests at the movie premiere.

Now that we were through with what was likely going to be the highlight of the tour, I figured I'd hit them with the historical part while I still had their attention. July tours could be a drag sometimes. All the TV shows were on vacation and the heat kept the few people working on movies indoors most of the day. Most of the two-hour Sovereign Studios walking tour was spent looking at the outsides of buildings while I talked about what went on inside. I had to parcel out the few highlights carefully so nobody got bored along the way.

"Sovereign Studios was formed in 1914 under the leadership of cousins, Harry and Max Burnbaum," I recited from memory as I led my tour group along the beige and red brick paseo at the front of the studio. "They started out in New York, but quickly moved out to Los Angeles, where the year-round nearly perfect weather was ideal for filming. . . ."

I guided my tour group through the studio's various office buildings at the front of the lot, explaining how each building is constructed in a different style of architecture, from Spanish Mission, to Victorian, to Modern. The building exteriors are all designed that way so they can be used in filming. Over the decades, every inch of Sovereign Studios has appeared in numerous movies and TV shows. The tourists get a kick out of figuring out what building has been used where.

As I finished my history on the building that houses the human resources offices— which is called "the castle" because of its palatial design—I saw that familiar mail cart with the familiar pirate flag heading in our direction once again. Sovereign Studios is large enough that I could usually go through an entire two-hour tour without running into a single friend. Figures that the one day there's someone I wanted to avoid, I couldn't *not* run into him.

"Let's go down here." I directed my group, taking an abrupt turn down an alley-way between the commissary and the child-care center. I'd never taken a tour down that particular road before, so I was struggling for something to say.

I looked over my shoulder in time to see the mail cart parking at the end of the alley. Since I couldn't go back, I would have to press on. Still with nothing to discuss about the most nondescript alleyway in the entire studio, I fell back on one of the tour games we rehearsed for just such an emergency to fill the silence.

"Does anyone know what their actor name would be?" I asked my tour group, and, once again, evoked looks of confusion. It used to be familiar practice for the studios to change an actor's name if it was too long or too ethnic or simply didn't fit. It still happens today. For instance, Natalie Portman's birth name is Natalie Hershlag.

"There's an old Hollywood tale," I told my tour, "about how actors used to come up with their stage names by using their middle name and the street they grew up on. In that case, my stage name would be Louise Lake. Sounds kind of old Hollywood, doesn't it? So, what would yours be?"

Naturally, my little Paris-in-training piped up first. "Ann Fremont," she said with an excited kind of glee.

"Joseph Brockton," another tourist called out.

"Christine Shisler," said a third.

Everyone in the group took a turn coming up with his or her stage name as we continued down the alley. We got stuck on a lady from New Jersey who had no middle name, and everyone chimed in with a suggestion of what to do. Ultimately we decided that she should go with a singular name like Madonna or Pink and we christened her "Magnolia."

That one not only gave us all a laugh, but the conversation carried us onto a main thoroughfare and back to the regularly scheduled tour. I continued to wind the group through the one hundred and fifty buildings that made up the Sovereign Studios lot as I told them more Hollywood stories. We didn't have any star sightings and weren't able to get onto any of the locked soundstages, but we did see the filming of a car commercial on the backlot. So the tour wasn't a total bust.

We ended in the studio store—or as I like to call it, the Bric-a-brac Shack. The tour is designed to begin and end at the shack so the studio has two chances to milk as much money out of the tourists as possible by selling them cheap key chains and other things they'd stick in a drawer the moment they got home. It's the same concept as Disneyland, where almost every ride ends in a souvenir shop.

I said my good-byes after Little Paris asked me to sign her autograph book. All in all, it was a pretty good tour considering it was a slow day on the lot. In my post-tour wind-down buzz, I'd totally forgotten about my near misses with the pirate mail cart until I walked out of the store and right into the driver's path.

Two

Personally, I think the sound of the screeching breaks was overkill. Sovereign Studios mail carts don't move that fast. Besides, I wasn't even in the cart's path, really.

"Tracy!" Mailroom Guy hopped out of the cart, shaking his unruly long brown hair out of his face. "You need to watch where you're walking."

"Yeah," I said in as noncommittal a tone as I could muster. Silly me for walking on a public thoroughfare.

"I guess you didn't see me earlier," he said. "I passed you on your tour a couple of times."

"Did you?" I asked, trying to sound surprised. "I didn't notice."

Mailroom Guy looked disappointed that he hadn't made more of an impression. By the way, Mailroom Guy's real name is Xanthe. My best friend, Liz, and I decided that he was far too bland for such an interesting name, so we call him Mailroom Guy . . . but not to his face.

I'd gone out with Mailroom Guy over the weekend. He'd taken me to this Pirate-themed dinner theater with a swashbuckling show and serving wenches and every pirate cliché I'd ever heard of in my life. I'm sure it could have been fun, but Mailroom Guy got *way* into the festivities, speaking in "pirate" with "Arghs!" and "Avast, ye mateys!" all night long. I should have known something was weird when he picked me up for the date wearing an eye patch.

"So," he said as he leaned an arm on his pirate-flag-draped mail cart. "I was thinking—"

"You know," I interrupted. I knew where this was going and I wanted to head it off quickly. "You were so much fun the other night. But I have to tell you, I have kind of a thing about pirates."

"What kind of thing?" he asked.

"It's kind of a fear," I said. "A phobia. It

goes back to the first time I saw Captain Hook from *Peter Pan*. Pirates terrify me. I can't even see Johnny Depp in any movie now."

I could tell that he was having a hard time wrapping his brain around the concept of pirates being scary. "Why didn't you say something?"

"You seemed so into the pirates," I said in a major understatement. Now that I was closer to his mail cart, I could see the inside was tricked out with an old-fashioned compass on the dash, a spyglass tied to the metal frame, and a trio of gold coins hanging from the rearview mirror.

"I am," he said with a solemn nod, knowing where this conversation was going.

"And I would never want to keep you from the thing you loved," I said. "So, maybe we should just be friends."

Mailroom Guy tried to protest, saying that he could cut back on his pirate fixation, but after a few rounds discussing our potential "future relationship" it was clear that this was too big a part of his life. He agreed that we weren't a good match and we decided to part as friends, which was good since I couldn't spend the rest of the summer altering my tour route to avoid him.

After he drove off in his cart, I remained standing along the paseo for a minute, wallowing in a minor bout of depression. Not that I missed Mailroom Guy or anything. I was kind of glad to have the whole thing over with so I could stop worrying about him. But Mailroom Guy was part of a bigger problem, one that I was doing my best trying to avoid dealing with as well.

I turned away from the departing cart and went to the cafeteria to grab a quick dinner and to shake off the bad feeling I had. I hated breaking up with guys. Even though one bad date hardly counted as a relationship, it was still hard to say "no thanks" when asked to go on a second. In spite of the fact that I'd been getting a lot of practice saying no to second dates lately, it was still an uncomfortable experience. I tried to put it out of my mind as I entered the Sovereign Studios commissary.

Liz had already gotten her food and grabbed us a table by the window overlooking the fountain on the paseo. I waved to her before turning into the serving area. This part of the commissary was cafeteria style, with one line for hot food and one for sandwiches. The formal dining room was on the other side of the building, separated by a glass wall that allowed us worker bees to look—but not touch—the executives and celebrities who regularly dined there. I didn't much mind. I'd seen the dining room menu once, and a simple hamburger would have cost me three hours' pay.

The dinner crowd wasn't nearly as bad as the lunch rush. The only people eating were the ones working or attending the premiere later. Normally, I'd be going home after my tours, but I'd agreed to pull a double and work the premiere. I never turned down the extra cash from working overtime.

Even though the place wasn't packed, I'd been on my feet all day and didn't feel like waiting in line for food. I grabbed a premade Asian chicken salad and a Sobe green tea out of the refrigerators, paid for them, and joined Liz at our table. She was busy writing in her journal.

"Revising?" I asked as I sat.

"Always," she said as she put down her pen. Liz had this incredible to-do list of experiences she wanted to have before she started cosmetology school in the fall. The list covered everything from crashing an A-list party to biking to San Francisco. There was no way she was going to get it all in before September, but the fun part was imagining it all up . . . at least as far as I was concerned. If you asked Liz, I'm sure she'd say she had more fun actually *doing* the stuff.

Liz was going to be a makeup artist and hairstylist for movies and TV, like her mom. Considering her mom's fame in that area, Liz knew she'd have no problem getting work right out of school, so this was her last summer "to experience life!" as she said. And, of course, she wanted to do all of it with her best friend alongside. Personally, I thought I was more suited to experience summer lounging by the pool, but I'd agreed to some of the less strenuous activities. But while she was planning to end the summer by going skydiving on her eighteenth birthday, I was going to lie back and watch her from the ground.

Somehow, I didn't think watching my best friend leap out of a plane at ten thousand feet was going to be nearly as relaxing as the pool.

"And Mailroom Guy bites the dust," I

announced while I poured dressing over my salad.

"I thought that was a good thing," she said. "Your mood's as blue as your blazer."

"And about as comfortable too," I replied as I slipped out of my uniform jacket. Sovereign Studios tour guides are made to wear the traditional page uniform at work: a blue polyester blazer, gray polyester pants, a white polyester shirt, and a blue tie. The tie is actually silk, but it's also a clip-on. So, any points the designer gets for the material choice are totally negated by the construction.

Liz was stuck in the same uniform, but she'd done some alterations that made it far more comfortable. It's amazing how a simple cut or a whole new lining will do wonders. The outfit still looked boringly bland as far as fashion statements went, but it was a ton lighter and more flexible than the scratchy polyester that I was bound in. I kept meaning to ask her to give my uniform the once-over.

"I think I'm in a funk," I said.

"A generic funk or something specific?"

"A guy funk," I said, taking a bite out of my salad.

"Ah," she said.

"There seems to be a pattern developing," I said, finally forcing myself to deal with the thing I'd been avoiding for weeks. "I D-Q'd Dairy Queen guy, slammed the book on the worm I met at Barnes & Noble, and couldn't even find an interesting way to describe how boring the dude from the surf shop was. All before we even got to a second date."

"You *have* been going on a lot of first dates lately," Liz said. "Not to say there's anything wrong with serial dating."

"Except for all the Froot Loops you meet along the way," I said. Like she knew anything about serial dating. She was a serial monogamist. The queen of relationships all through middle school and high school. At the start of every school year, she'd begin dating a new guy. It would be months of bliss, until about mid-April when the guy realized that—after spending every weekend hiking through the Santa Monica mountains, skiing in Big Bear, and dirt-bike riding in the desert—going out with Liz could be exhausting.

Every guy she ever dated tended to break up with her before the year was out. She kept saying how she didn't mind since she liked to take the summers for herself, but I knew that she was ready for a serious *long*, long-term thing, even though she hadn't turned eighteen yet.

I understood how she felt. I'd never had a real relationship before. Sure, I'd had boyfriends. I'd been going out with a real sweet guy named Scott at the start of senior year. He was the longest relationship I've ever had, and we didn't even make it to Christmas. After a while we both realized there was no spark and ended it . . . blandly.

The first-date syndrome seemed to be a recent development. In my post-Scott world I was so busy getting ready to graduate from high school and start my life that guys always seemed to take the backseat. It was almost like I would give up on a date before I'd even started, because none of those guys seemed to fit my picture for the future. I wasn't in some great rush to settle down or anything, but I wasn't really seeing the point of random dating when everything else I was doing was planning for the long term. Not that I had any clue what my life held in store for me beyond college. I hadn't even settled on a major yet.

"If only these dates were . . . more, well, just more," I said.

"Not every first date can be a candlelit dinner at the Griffith Observatory," Liz said.

"True," I agreed with a sigh.

Liz was talking about what my parents did on their first date. Dad was an astronomy student at the time. He'd given up an entire month of his life to help one of his professors rewrite the manuscript for a textbook about the universe. The professor's editors had hated the first draft.

After Dad gave it the once-over, it was accepted by the publisher and much congratulations were heaped on the professor for the amazing work he'd done revising it. The professor thanked Dad by getting him access to the famous Griffith Observatory after hours so he could take the woman who would one day become my mom there on a date. Spending an evening alone together looking at the cosmos is a pretty impressive way to start off a relationship.

And it was just the inspiration I needed.

"I think it's time I fell in love," I declared, slamming down my bottle of Sobe tea to punctuate the statement. It felt like the moment required a dramatic action. We *were* at a movie studio after all.

"Always a good way to pass the time," Liz agreed with a smile. That smile dropped when she saw the look on my face and realized I was being serious. "Tracy?"

"Hear me out," I said. "I'm spending so much time thinking about the future that I'm missing out on the present. And the thing I've been missing out on most is a good guy. I've got to stop worrying about all that future stuff and just let myself fall in love."

Liz nodded. "Okay, yes, that's a good point," she said. "But should falling in love really be a goal? It's not something to put on a to-do list."

"You know what I mean," I said. "I don't have to worry about school until the fall. I don't have to worry about my future until after that. I can spend my summer finding the perfect love."

Liz cocked her ear like she was listening for something.

"What are you doing?" I asked.

"Waiting for the music to swell," she said. "If this were a movie, this would be the point where the sappy romantic music hits a crescendo."

I flicked a sesame seed at her.

"Ladies!" a familiar male voice said from behind me.

"Hey, bro!" I said as Dex sat beside me. Technically, he was Liz's brother, but I'd been calling him "bro" since before I found out it was actually lame to call anyone "bro," and it kind of stuck. "Thanks for the light effects earlier. The tourists got a kick out of it."

"Anytime," he said with a smile. "Now maybe you can help *me*. I've got a bet with the guys on the light crew. I need to know what the first movie to win the Academy Award for Best Picture was. They're telling me it was a Sovereign Studios film."

"Ha!" Liz and I spat out in unison. Even in its earliest days, Sovereign Studios was never known for quality films. Huge money-making blockbusters? Yes. But award-winning works of art? Not even.

"I've got a case of Jones soda riding on it," Dex said. "Bubblegum flavor."

"Eww," I said, sticking out my tongue. "Too sweet."

"Thanks," he said. "You're sweet too."

I smacked him on the shoulder. Dex was actually the first of the Sanchez siblings that

I had met back in kindergarten. He and Liz are twins. They look a lot alike actually, with the same straight black hair and green eyes, and this beautifully tanned skin they get along with their Mexican heritage.

Dex and I probably would have become best friends the moment he offered me his chocolate milk on the first day. I mean, come on, he was gifting me with chocolate! But he was a yucky boy so it was only natural that Liz and I would be friends while he followed us around pretending to hate us.

"Wait a minute," Liz said. "A bunch of union guys made a bet for bubblegum flavored soda?"

Dex blushed. "Well . . . if they win I give them beer money. If I win I get bubblegum soda."

His sister tried her best not to laugh. She failed.

Dex is only an apprentice in the studio's lighting department since he just got out of high school. He's not a full-scale union guy, but he doesn't really want to be doing that for the rest of his life like most of his coworkers have been. He'd much rather be an actor. Dex took the job because his dad works on the studio's light crew and Dex needed the money for college. The guys are always making fun of him because he's so young.

"You know the answer, right?" Dex asked.

I stole a french fry off his plate. "The first film to win an Academy Award was *Wings*. It was produced by Paramount Pictures in 1927."

Dex gave his fist a pump in the air. "Yes! I can't wait to tell those guys. I will totally split the soda with you."

"That's okay," I said. *Really*.

"So, what was the topic of conversation before I got here?"

"Tracy and her guy problems," Liz said casually.

"Liz!" I shouted through clenched teeth. Luckily the teeth clenching and the volume of the conversations around us kept my voice from carrying.

"What?" Liz asked, all innocent-like. "If you can't talk to your brother-substitute about guy troubles, who can you talk to?"

But I wasn't about to talk to anyone about anything, because at that very moment the door to the commissary opened and *he* walked in.

If my life were a movie, this would be

the part where the film went into slow motion as the dusty blond–haired, blue-eyed, stylishly-dressed-in-a-suit-two-levels-above-his-pay-grade guy of my dreams entered the picture: Connor Huxley.

Connor was a summer intern in the motion picture marketing department. I'd met him when I gave the orientation tour on his first day at the studio. Every Monday a tour guide takes the new employees around to give them a little background on the studio and point out the necessary places, like the commissary, credit union, infirmary—that kind of thing. Sovereign Studios covers over seventy-five acres in the heart of Hollywood so it's not like your typical office place. New employees can get lost just looking for a bathroom.

During the one hour mini-tour, I learned that Connor was going into his sophomore year at USC as a marketing major. We hit it off pretty well in spite of the fact that I was about to start at UCLA in the fall, which made us natural enemies because of our rival school choices.

We'd both been so busy with our summer jobs that we'd hardly talked since then, other than saying "Hi" as we passed while I was giving a tour or he was running an errand. A couple of times I thought he was going to ask me out, but then a tourist interrupted, or he got a call from his boss on his cell phone and had to run off. I thought about asking him out too, but considering how unlucky I'd been with love lately, I didn't see the point.

"Where did she go?" Dex asked, waving his hand in front of my face.

"I don't know," Liz replied. "But she always goes there when Connor's around."

I had a sneaking suspicion that they were talking about me. "Excuse me?"

"You're all dreamy-eyed," Liz said.

"I am *not* dreamy-eyed," I replied, blinking pointedly at her. "I was thinking."

"About *Coooonnor*," Liz said in a singsong voice that made both Dex and me roll our eyes.

"Him again?" Dex asked. He always hated when we got all girly, talking about guys. I guess there are some subjects guys are uncomfortable about hearing from their sisters—or sister-substitutes.

"Abrupt subject switch," I announced, hoping to derail the topic of conversation before it got started. "Do we know how long this movie's supposed to run? I don't want to be stuck on VIP transport all night."

"You got shuttle duty?" Liz asked. "That sucks."

"One of the biggest movie premieres of the summer and I'm stuck driving the guests back and forth from the theater to the dining room all night, and I don't even get to see the movie."

"But you probably get to meet celebs," Dex said. "Maybe hang with Christy Caldwell."

"Ha!" Liz and I said—again—in unison. We'd both done VIP transport before. We knew full well that shuttle duty was the last place anyone got to interact with the glamorous glitterati.

"The celebrities all get personal handlers escorting them," I explained to Dex. "Shuttle duty is for the executives who think they're somebody—"

"Well, technically, they *are* somebody," Liz said. "They do kind of run the studio."

"What are you doing for the premiere?" Dex asked his biological sister.

"Ushering," she replied. "Which means I'm stuck inside watching this drivel."

Dex shook his head. "What is it with you two? We get to work at Sovereign Studios, one of the oldest motion picture and TV lots in Hollywood." He looked at me. "You're going to be rubbing elbows with some of the biggest power players in town—"

"More like carting their butts around."

He turned to his sister. "And you're going to be one of the first people in the world to see what everyone is saying will be the blockbuster romantic comedy of the summer. You are both way too young to be so jaded."

"When did he become the voice of reason?" I asked Liz.

"Always been that way," Liz replied. "It's damn annoying."

Dex was right, though. And we weren't seriously upset about working the premiere. We just like to whine sometimes. It was kind of exciting to be involved in a big movie premiere with movie stars and the Hollywood elite—even if I was nothing more than a second-rate chauffeur. But you never want to *look* like you're excited about those things. That would be tacky.

Jaded is the Hollywood version of excitement.

"Are you sticking around for the premiere?" I asked Dex.

"Can't," he said. "I've got an audition for a play in a little theater on Santa Monica."

"Break a leg," I said. I wanted to ask him more about it, but Dex didn't like talking about roles until he had them. Like everyone else in Hollywood, Dex had aspirations for something beyond his day job. Well, like everyone but me. I still wasn't sure what I wanted to be when I grew up, but I knew that tour guide was not a career option. At least Dex wasn't going the typical route of being a waiter while he pursued his acting dreams.

"Hey," Liz said. "Here comes lover boy again."

I willed myself not to look up from my salad, but I could see Liz's body shift as she turned toward the kitchen. I silently repeated to myself, *Don't look. Don't look.* But the salad could only hold my interest for so long.

My head popped up to catch a glimpse of Connor as he elbowed his way out the door of the commissary. He was loaded down with about a half dozen to-go containers, heading back to the office with his bosses' meals, I guessed. I bet I'd see him at the premiere later.

Suddenly, my outlook on the event was a lot less jaded.

Three

I had to wonder if VIP transport duty was assigned as some kind of punishment, except I hadn't done anything wrong. The premiere of one of the summer's biggest movies was taking place at the studio entrance, with stars and paparazzi and huge crowds of fans. Yet I was stuck on a tour cart in the back of the theater along with a pair of my coworkers who spent the entire time debating what Hollywood clubs had the highest celebrity sighting ratio.

The three of us were lined up in the studio's sleek black tour carts that we usually used for the VIP tours. They sat eight people, uncomfortably, and were designed to be all cool and trendy, but they pretty much looked like golf carts with a shiny paint job . . . which is what they were.

I'd worked three movie premieres the previous summer, but *Table for Two* was my first of the new season. The awe I'd initially felt working a premiere disappeared quickly when I found out at the first one that most of the guests don't actually stick around to watch the movie. They walk down the red carpet, have their picture taken by the paparazzi as they enter the theater, then slip out the back where members of the marketing and publicity team whisk them away to the party before the poor pages can even get a good look at them. Then again, most of the celebs had already seen the movie at least once in prescreenings, so it wasn't like they were missing anything.

I checked my watch. It was only five minutes after eight. Way too early for anyone to sneak out yet. The premiere was scheduled to begin at eight o'clock on the dot, which translates into roughly eight-thirty Hollywood time.

I pulled one of my curls down in front of my eyes to examine my hair, like I usually do when I'm bored. There was no real reason for it. My hair was fine. It looked like it always did; perfectly healthy in tight brown curls. I was annoyed with myself for forgetting to bring a book to read.

"Anything interesting there?" asked a voice that clearly did not belong to the other pages.

I released the curl and it sprung back out of my eyesight. Connor, the costar of my movie-themed fantasies was standing beside me. "Oh . . . um . . . I didn't see you."

I looked past him and saw a few of the marketing and publicity interns standing around the back door to the theater. They'd taken position to intercept the celebrities and zip them off to the party once they made their escape. We lowly pages couldn't be trusted with the A-List, I guess. Then again, having already spent the past fifteen minutes listening to my cohorts regale everyone in the vicinity with their star-stalking stories, I could kind of understand why the studio might feel that way.

"You seemed very intent on your hair," he said, leaning an arm on the metal bar that held up the roof of the cart. "Thinking of a change?"

"Why? Do you think I need to change it?" Way to be secure, there.

"No!" he said. "I meant . . . you seemed so focused."

"Just daydreaming," I said. "It gets kind of boring back here where the action isn't."

"What?" he whispered. "Ric isn't keeping you entertained with his tales of the wild night he spent partying with Lindsay Lohan?"

I choked out a laugh, turning at the same time to make sure my coworker, Ric, hadn't heard Connor. He was too busy watching his friend Tessa do her Britney Spears impression.

"I thought he only annoyed the other pages with those stories," I whispered back to Connor.

"He tells anyone who will listen. I was stuck in line behind him at the ATM last payday. By the time we worked our way to the front he'd dropped more names than Joan Rivers working the red carpet. Although he managed to get most of the names right, unlike Joan."

I laughed a little harder than I felt the joke warranted, then worried that I was trying too hard and toned the chuckling down. It faded out pathetically with a kind of wheezing noise that I hoped he didn't notice.

I don't usually get nervous around guys, but this was *Connor* and I'd just decided that he was possibly my best chance at a relationship before school started in a month. The only problem was that I had no clue how to go about letting him know that. In the meantime, he was standing in front of me and I didn't want to waste the opportunity. I flashed him my brightest and most flirtatious smile and waited to see what would happen.

"Um . . . ," he said. "I was asked to . . . um . . . ask you guys to move your carts so we can park here. It's a more convenient spot to pick up the cast and special guests so we can get them to the party."

"Oh," I said. That was why he came over. How disappointing. My smile couldn't help but falter. "Okay."

"Thanks," Connor said. "That's great."

He shifted on his feet but he didn't walk away. He didn't say anything either. Neither did I.

I couldn't believe that we finally had a few minutes to talk and neither one of us could think of a thing to say. I didn't entirely blame myself, what with the whole major life realization I had just made at dinner. My mind was cluttered with ideas on the proper way to go about falling in love. All that confusion made it hard to figure out what to say to actually start the "courting process."

But what was *his* problem, I wondered.

"So . . . have you seen the movie yet?" Connor asked.

"Table for Two?" I asked. Like he'd be talking about any other movie. "No. Not yet. You?"

"A few times," he said. "I sat in on some of the screenings."

"Oh," I said. "What did you think?"

"It's better now," Connor said. "The latest version of the movie scored a ninety-eight percent positive rating. That's, like, the most popular a Sovereign film has ever been with a test audience. Course it helped when we changed the ending."

I didn't comment on the "we" in his sentence. I doubed that he had anything to do with the new ending. Interns don't tend to have that kind of power.

I'd heard rumors that the original ending had been changed because test audiences didn't like that the main character, played by Hollywood It Girl Christy Caldwell, wound up alone. I got to read an early draft of the script and thought that it was a great way to end the film. Far more realistic than most romantic comedies. But what audience goes to that kind of movie expecting the lead to end up single? Sure, it worked in *My Best Friend's Wedding*, but that was Julia Roberts. As long as she gets to keep her hair down and smile throughout a film she can sell any ending.

"You've got to see it," Connor said. "I could still go see it again . . . um . . . I mean . . . it's so good that I could see it again and again."

I wasn't sure if he'd just asked me on a date, but his nervousness was kind of cute.

Normally in these situations, I'd take it upon myself to save the guy the struggle and ask him out. I'm not usually one to play coy and make a guy jump through hoops. I have no problem making the first move.

But I couldn't stop thinking what the point would be of another boring first date with no sparks. I didn't want Connor to become my next Mailroom Guy or whatever. It was bad enough that I had to avoid the mailroom because of a bad date. Pretty soon, half the lot would be off-limits to me.

I wanted to get him to love me. And, more importantly, I wanted to find a way to love him. And none of that was going to happen if we just went out for a boring dinner and a movie. We needed something special. I needed some kind of plan.

And I had no idea what that plan would be.

As Connor shifted from one foot to the other, I began to hope that he would shift himself away from me. I wasn't ready for another bad date, and there was no point in accepting his invitation until I figured out a way to fix my funk.

"Well . . . um . . . see ya," Connor said.

Still, he didn't move.

"Yeah," I replied, wishing that he would both stay *and* go. "Later."

Connor nodded deeply a few times, then went back to his friends standing by the theater door. I gave myself a mental kick in the head. There was no guarantee that a date with Connor would end horribly. I could have just blown my chance at that relationship I was looking for.

I pulled another coil of hair down in front of my eyes. There was still a good twenty minutes before I'd be put into service and now I had to spend it with Connor awkwardly trying not to look at me.

Then I remembered that he needed us to move.

"Guys," I said, trying to get Ric and Tessa's attention. "We have to—"

The rear door of the Sovereign Theater slammed open, scaring everyone in the vicinity. By the time I realized where the noise had come from, the interns were already scrambling to the door and blocking my view. I'd only caught a glimpse of the phantom slammer.

It couldn't have been who I thought it was.

I checked my watch. It was still way too early for anyone to be slipping out before the movie started. Something must have gone wrong inside and one of the executives was coming out to get help from the interns. The fact that she looked like Christy Caldwell had to be a coincidence. It could not possibly have been the actress herself.

Still, from all the scrambling interns in front of me, it did look like the world was coming to an end.

Finally, the sea of interns parted and I

could get a better look at who had come out of the theater. It wasn't a studio executive. It was exactly who I'd thought it was.

Christy Caldwell, star of stage, screen, and Clairol commercials, was pushing her way through the throng of interns. She nearly knocked Connor into a bush as she passed. . . .

And made her way straight toward me.

Four

"Drive," Christy Caldwell—*The* Christy Caldwell—said as she slipped into the seat beside me.

"I'm sorry?" I asked. Christy Caldwell did not just hop into my cart and tell me to drive. Couldn't happen. I must have fallen asleep while I was playing with my hair.

"I said drive," Christy repeated. "*Please.*"

I turned to the actress beside me. Nope. She was there. It wasn't a dream.

Christy Caldwell was even more beautiful in person than on-screen, if that was even possible. She was wearing a stunning floral print summer dress that hung perfectly on her body. She was thin, but not sickly looking, which you don't often see in

Hollywood starlets. I couldn't even make out one rib through the dress. Her skin was flawlessly perfect and her blond hair was so straight that I think my curls tightened a little in envy when they saw it.

I'd seen several celebrities since I started working at Sovereign Studios. I'd run into Angelina Jolie walking along the paseo with an entourage in which everyone wore matching dark sunglasses. George Clooney once passed by in a chauffeur-driven electric cart. And I swear I'd even seen Dakota Fanning giving a studio executive a stern talking-to. But all of those sightings were at a distance, while I tried to keep my tour group moving so they didn't stop and stare. This was the first time I'd actually interacted with a star. To be perfectly honest, it was kind of freaking me out.

I looked over to Connor and his friends. They were whispering to each other like they didn't know what to do. I could relate.

"But, the interns are supposed to—"

"I am sick of the sycophants," Christy said. "I need some air."

I looked back to the sycophants. The interns still hadn't taken a step toward us.

There was no way this was going to end

well for me. Either I upset one of the biggest stars in Hollywood by ignoring her, or I make a bunch of studio execs mad by listening to her and helping her ditch the premiere early. The studio execs would have the easier time getting me fired, but there was something about the pleading way that Christy was looking at me that made my decision.

With a shrug, I turned the key of the electric cart's ignition. "Okay," I said. "Do you want to go to the party?"

"No chance," Christy replied. "Take me someplace away."

"Away where?"

"Away from everything."

"I don't think the electric cart has enough of a charge to get that far."

Christy laughed, which helped put me a bit more at ease. "Just take me someplace where nobody will annoy me," she said.

I considered dazzling the starlet with another witty response, but I didn't want to press my luck. I threw the cart into drive and pulled away. Connor stood there with a smirk and waved while his friends panicked around him. I took it as a good sign.

I veered to the right and drove between

the administration building and Stage 1, successfully avoiding the front of the theater and the paparazzi-lined red carpet. The last thing I needed was to appear on the cover of all the tabloids under the headline:

AMERICA'S SWEETHEART THROWS TANTRUM, DITCHES PREMIERE!
Unidentified Page with Frizzy Hair
Aids in Escape

The tabloids can be cruel sometimes.

I reviewed the studio map in my head as I drove. We had to commit the thing to memory back during tour training. There were plenty of places to hide all over the lot—in storage rooms under buildings, or in rarely visited back corners way off the tour path. None of them seemed the right place to take America's Sweetheart.

"Are you sure you don't want to go to the commissary for the party, Ms. Caldwell?" I asked as we drove past the costume building.

"You're like, what?" she asked. "A couple of years younger than me?"

I wasn't sure where she was going with the question, but I considered telling her I was exactly three years and two days younger than her. I try to learn everything I can about the celebrities in Sovereign Studios' movies. It makes the tours more interesting, which sometimes gets me tips. But going into all that I knew about her would probably make me seem a wee bit stalkerish, and that was probably the last thing she needed at the moment.

"It's bad enough when the senior executives call me by my last name," the actress said. "Makes me feel like I'm a little girl being scolded. But it's worse when people my own age kowtow to me. Call me Christy. All I want is to be Christine Lifshiltz for five minutes."

"Okay, Christy," I said. I wondered if she'd grown up on a Caldwell Street somewhere and that was how she came by her stage name. "But someone's going to be looking for you."

"How 'bout you make sure they don't find me?"

"Will do," I said, turning left at the scene shop with no clear idea where I was going. Since it was well after regular work hours, the lot was much less crowded than usual, but the place never really shut down. We passed several people straining to catch a glimpse of Christy as we went by. Celebrities don't usually hang around the backlot area unless they're filming.

Even with only a skeleton crew working, there was no way I could just drive around with Christy Caldwell-Lifshiltz in my cart without anyone noticing.

"I've got an idea," I said, turning into the New York backlot, where we were transported to another world . . . or at least, another city. The multipurpose office buildings and oversized soundstages were gone. We were surrounded by rows of brick and stone buildings that mimicked neighborhoods in Manhattan, Brooklyn, and those other boroughs I've never been to.

It was all Hollywood magic, of course. There wasn't a single brick or stone on any of the streets. Every building was nothing more than a facade, a false front made of fiberglass. One of the highlights of the studio tour was letting the tourists knock on the fake brick so they could hear the hollow echo.

I parked the cart behind a Dumpster where I hoped no one would accidentally stumble across it.

"They'll never think to look for me

here," Christy said, holding her hand over her nose.

"We're ditching the cart," I explained. "Follow me."

Christy didn't waste any time asking questions as I hopped out of the cart and walked up the stairs of the nearest brownstone. She followed willingly and I was glad that I had somehow earned her trust.

The front door to the fake brownstone wasn't locked. None of the doors on the street ever were since there was nothing behind them to steal. I checked to make sure no one was watching us, then slipped inside.

There was no foyer or living room on the other side of the door. The interior was empty except for support beams, a staircase, and a concrete wall supporting the facade. All the other front doors on the row of houses opened into the same dark, cavernous spot.

"This way," I said as I started up the stairs.

I'd only been up those stairs once before. It was during our first week of training more than a year earlier. One of the senior tour guides had asked me out on a date to go stargazing after work. At first, I'd thought he meant that he was going to take me to some Hollywood hot spot to see celebrities. I was kind of embarrassed when he had to explain that he was talking about the actual stars in the sky.

Even then, I'd thought he meant we were going to the Griffith Observatory, like my parents had done on their first date. I didn't think we'd have the place to ourselves or anything, but it seemed like a good start. It never crossed my mind that we'd be going to the roof of some fake building in the middle of the place we worked. Still, I was game for it when I saw the blanket laid out. A picnic under the stars would have been quite a romantic first date.

Then I realized that there was no food. Only a blanket. And I was pretty sure from the way he was looking at me that my date had other plans for the evening. I turned around and left the roof, slamming the door behind me.

Was it my fault that the door locked and the poor guy was stuck up there until the next morning? He *did* have a blanket to keep him warm.

"Glad I'm not in heels," Christy said,

interrupting my thoughts, as we made our way to the top of the four-story fake building.

I pushed the door open and we exited out onto the roof. It wasn't quite the tallest building on the lot, but it still had a great view, and the added bonus that no one would ever think to look for us up there.

I made sure to prop the door open so that there was no repeat of my lame date's fate. Didn't need to get stuck on the roof with Christy Caldwell. With the sun setting, it was getting chilly and Christy was only wearing a thin slip dress. Obviously, neither of us had thought to bring a blanket.

"Wow," Christy said as she looked out at the fading sun. "Hollywood looks almost nice from up here."

"Just don't turn to your left," I warned. Our little slice of movie magic was an island of tranquility in a rather sketchy neighborhood by most standards.

"So, what's your name, anyway?" Christy asked.

In all the excitement I hadn't had the chance to introduce myself. "Tracy," I said. "Tracy Vance."

"Well, Tracy Vance, it's very nice to meet you." Christy held out a hand and I quickly took it. This was the first celebrity hand I'd ever shaken. Not surprisingly, Christy's hand felt no different from anyone else's hand that I'd ever shaken, though her skin was incredibly smooth. I imagine that was from the free spa days she was probably offered all over town so owners could tell people that Christy Caldwell was their client.

Christy turned back out to look over the studio. All the lights were coming on around us as the sun faded in the west.

While her back was to me, I stole a glance over toward the theater. It was a couple of blocks away from us, but I could see that the crowd was finally making its way inside. What I couldn't see were the search parties that must have been sent out to find the star of the movie. But just because I couldn't see them didn't mean they weren't all over the lot.

I am so *getting fired for this,* I thought.

"Are you sure you don't want to go to the party?" I suggested. "Or maybe back to the theater?"

Christy let out her signature laugh. It's been described as a cross between a giggle and titter. *Entertainment Weekly* claims that it's an important part of why she can now ask for twelve million dollars per film. It *is* kind of infectious. I know I felt like laughing right then.

So fired.

Now that we had a moment to breathe, it finally hit me that I was hanging with Christy Caldwell, Movie Star! It wasn't exactly the hard partying lifestyle I'd imagined for a celebrity, but since she first hopped into my cart things certainly hadn't been dull.

Actually, Christy doesn't have the party girl reputation of some of her contemporaries, but she does lead an interesting life. She is only a few years older than me and she's already traveled the world and dined at the White House. I was dying to ask her what we were hiding from, but I didn't want to pry.

Okay. I *totally* wanted to pry, but I didn't want her to get mad at me and leave in a huff that would ensure that I got fired.

"I guess you've already seen *Table for Two?*" I asked, assuming that she'd seen a screening, which is why she didn't mind missing the premiere.

"Please, I've lived it," Christy said as she

leaned against the ledge. "This is my third romantic comedy in a row. I keep asking my agent to get me a dramatic role. Maybe a period piece. Put me in a corset and I can win an Oscar. But no. My fans want a light comedy. Don't want to have to deal with reality. Don't want me to put my hair up in a bun."

I could understand that last part. She has really great hair. "But they were all smash hits. Weren't they?"

"Of course they were," Christy said. "This one will be too. It's the same story! Girl meets boy. Girl loses boy. Girl gets boy back. Lather. Rinse. Repeat."

"Well, yeah, they are a little formulaic."

"A little?"

"But the audience likes them. They keep coming back."

"Because the audience likes happy endings. Who wouldn't want to fall in love the way I did in the last one. Did you see it?"

"You mean *How to Get Over Heartbreak in Ten Easy Steps*?" I asked, pretending I wasn't sure what she was talking about even though I'd seen it twice in the theater and bought it on DVD the first day it was out.

"That one's my favorite title," she said.

"And it's the perfect example. Ten *easy* steps are all it takes to find love again. Because there's no love like movie love."

"Well, there *is* no love like movie love," I said.

And like Liz had said at dinner, if this had been a scene in a movie, this is the point where the music would swell and the camera would push in to a tight close-up of my face. The audience would be able to tell from the glimmer of light—that a visual effects artist added in the corner of my eye—that the movie star had just given me a brilliant idea.

The sides of my mouth would curl into a wicked little smile.

Then, there'd be an abrupt cut to the next scene.

If this were a movie.

Five

The next morning, I was already heading to the door when the doorbell rang at the same moment my cell phone buzzed. The screen on my cell told me that Liz was on the line, so I let it go to voicemail. I had totally bailed on her at the premiere and hadn't had the chance to explain why. My apology for that needed to be face-to-face, because it's harder to hang up on someone standing in front of you.

Although, honestly, it wasn't my fault that Christy wanted to spend so much time chatting up on the roof, no matter how chilly it got. We finally climbed down about an hour after the movie had started. Since the bulk of shuttle duty was done for the night, my boss, Carl, sent me home after giving me grief about abandoning my post. Thankfully, Christy had come along to explain why I'd disappeared, which was very helpful to me keeping my job since Carl is a major fan of hers.

Since Liz was still stuck in the theater for another hour, I went home without saying good-bye. I'd planned to call her and tell her everything that had happened, but I got so caught up in the plan that Christy had unknowingly inspired that I lost all track of time. It was well after midnight before I noticed that Liz had left a pair of messages on my cell phone.

The doorbell rang again, pulling me out of my musings.

"I got it!" I called out to Mom as I opened the front door. A delivery guy was standing there holding a huge bouquet of wildflowers. "It's for you, Mom!"

"Special occasion?" the delivery guy asked as he handed me a sheet to sign for the flowers.

"Nope. Just Wednesday," I said as I reached for the table beside the door where we kept the tip jar and pulled out a couple of bucks. "You must be new."

The guy had this adorably perplexed look on his face. I doubt he would have thought his new floral delivery route had regulars. After a while on the job, I was sure we'd be getting to know him quite well, just as we had with his predecessor.

Mom came up behind me as I was delicately trying to unload the overflowing arrangement from his arms.

"Your father is so thoughtful," Mom said, taking the flowers from me and flashing the delivery guy her brightest smile. "I guess John got that job with FedEx."

"Yeah," he said, squinting in confusion. "I started over the weekend."

"Well, welcome," Mom said as she closed the door. "See you again soon."

"Oh, okay," he said, as he walked back to his delivery van.

I took a moment to fawn over the beautiful arrangement, gave my mom a kiss good-bye and took off for Liz's house, waving good-bye to the delivery guy as he started up his van. I could tell he was still trying to wrap his brain around the idea of a man sending his wife flowers for no reason at all. But that's the kind of guy my dad is.

Mom would thank him later with some

equally thoughtful token. Then the whole thing would start up again in a couple of days when one of them did something incredibly romantic for the other. My parents have the kind of love that people write about.

Seriously.

There are a handful of scripts that have been making their way around Hollywood for decades, but haven't been made into movies for one reason or another. One of them was written by my dad's college roommate, who was also the best man at his wedding. I call him Uncle Earl.

Good ol' Uncle Earl has the script for one of the most romantic movies of all time. It's called *True Love*, which is a fitting title, if a bit lackluster. The script opens with a couple that meets in college and has their first date at the Griffith Observatory, and it just gets more achingly romantic from there. Everyone who reads it immediately tears up, swoons, and gets little heart flutters. No movie studio has bought it because it's just too perfect a love story to be a believable movie.

And to think, it's based on my parents. Try living up to that romance sometime.

I know I'm lucky to have two parents

who are still as deeply in love with each other as they were when they got together, but sometimes I want them to have a real good screaming fight or something, if only to prove that they're not totally perfect.

I pulled out of the driveway in my little Honda and drove over to Liz's house, making a couple of stops along the way. We didn't live that far from each other, but between my stops and typical midday traffic it took me about an hour to get there. Since we both had pulled a double the day before, we had Wednesday off. I hoped that Liz didn't have any plans because I was going to need her help to do what I had in mind.

I also hoped that she would answer the door as I stood there ringing the bell. I'd been walking into her house ever since we both lived on Lake Street when we were kids. This was the first time I'd found the door locked to me.

I rang again.

"We don't want any!" Liz's voice called through the door.

"I brought movies!" I yelled back, holding up my bag. "And microwave popcorn! Extra butter!"

The door swung open. "You think you can

buy me off with that? You bailed on me last night. I never had the chance to tell you how Christy Caldwell totally stepped on my foot as she made her way down the red carpet."

"I think you'll forgive me when I tell you about my run-in with your foot-stomper," I said.

She still looked annoyed, but I could tell her curiosity was piqued. With a huff, she let me in, grabbing the box of popcorn out of my hand.

We adjourned to the kitchen where Liz popped the popcorn while I gave her a stellar recap of the night before, embellishing a few points to add to the drama. She listened intently as I described every moment, from my awkward conversation with Connor to my fleeing with the hottest celeb du jour.

We were so into the story that we didn't even notice the smell of burning popcorn until it was way too late to save a kernel. Liz took the bag out of the microwave and threw it right in the trash while I wrapped up my story.

"You are *so* lucky Carl didn't fire you," Liz said.

Not the response I was hoping for.

"What was I supposed to do?" I asked as

she put another bag of popcorn in the microwave, knocking thirty seconds off the timer. "Tie her to the hood of the cart and roll her back down the red carpet?"

"Fair point," Liz said as she started the microwave. "So what does one talk about with a big name celebrity?"

"Her movies," I said. "And movies in general. But she totally gave me this great idea. Christy was saying—"

"Oh, now it's *Christy*. Are you two new best friends for life? No wonder you couldn't be bothered to call me. I've been replaced!" Liz broke out into huge, melodramatic, and ridiculously fake sobs. She threw herself against the cabinet and pounded on it.

"Liz!"

"Go on," she said, pulling herself back together with the greatest of ease.

"Okay, so these romantic comedies the studio keeps popping out, they're all the same, right?"

"Painfully so."

"Well, there's got to be a reason, right? People see some kind of truth in them."

"Figures an airhead like Christy would say something like that to defend her work."

"Actually, she said exactly the opposite," I said. "This one is my airhead idea."

"In that case, go on," Liz said, waving me forward with my story.

"The point is, whether they're real or not, they're like the perfect setting for romance. The girl always gets her guy and they live happily ever after, right?"

"At least until the sequel," Liz said. "When one of the actors holds out for more money and then they recast, forcing the girl to fall for a whole different guy."

"You're not helping," I said.

"I'm not sure what it is you're asking me to help you with," Liz said. "Do you want to write a movie? 'Cause writing is so not my thing."

"No," I said. "I want to *live* one."

Liz paused for a moment to think about what I was saying. In that pause, the microwave dinged, signaling that the popcorn was ready. The lack of burning smell was a good indicator that the timing had been right this time. She didn't move to check it, though.

"Go on," she prodded skeptically.

"I'm going to follow the formula of all

those romantic comedies out there," I explained. "From the opening sequence to the final credits, they all stick to a basic pattern. I can use that pattern to plot out a relationship with Connor."

"Trap him in a relationship, you mean," Liz said as she took the popcorn bag out of the microwave, carefully opened it, and poured the contents into a bowl on the counter. A bunch of the kernels remained unpopped, but it was better than burned. She grabbed the bowl and went for the stairs.

I dutifully followed. I had to. If I was going to pull this off I was going to need her help.

"It's not trapping him," I said as we reached her bedroom. "Think of it as a creative form of dating. All I'm going to do is set up a romantic scenario and let it play out. I can't help it if he falls truly, madly, and deeply in love with me in the process."

Liz took another pause to think about what I was saying. Two pauses in only a few minutes meant I was wearing her down.

"And how do you intend to put this plan of yours into action?" Liz asked.

"Does that mean you're in?"

"No," Liz replied. "It means I need a good laugh. And this is the funniest idea I've heard in a long time."

I plopped down on her bed. "You're not taking this seriously."

She threw some popcorn at me. "Of course I'm not taking this seriously! It's supposed to be a comedy. I'm the wacky sidekick."

"Joking aside," I said to her, "you're going to help?"

"Well . . . ," she said, drawing out the suspense. "I reserve the right to be skeptical. . . ."

"Naturally."

"But it seems fairly harmless," she said. "Besides, it could be fun. I can add 'Help Tracy on a Madcap Adventure' to my to-do list. Where do we start?"

"Research." I opened the bag and spilled it out between us. A pile of DVDs poured onto the blanket. I'd cleaned out the romantic comedy section of the video store on the way over to Liz's house. There were about a dozen DVDs starring my new best friend, Christy Caldwell; as well as the Grande Dame of the Ro Com, Julia Roberts; the Lady in Waiting, Reese Witherspoon; and the Princess in Training,

Anne Hathaway. Throw in some Mandy Moore and Lindsay Lohan for a little battle of good versus evil, and we covered every romantic cliché known to womankind. It was going to be *great*.

Liz looked down at the pile. "You want to watch all those today?"

"I never said this was going to be easy."

"Okay," Liz said. "But I draw the line at Hilary Duff."

"Don't we all," I said. This was getting exciting. I had expected it to take a lot more work to convince Liz to go along with my plan. I guess she realized that I was determined to do this whether or not she went along. It was a good thing we got that part over with quickly, because the next thing I was about to suggest was going to be way harder to convince her of.

"You have that look," she said to me, "like there's something else."

"Well . . ." I reached into my bag again. I felt a little like Mary Poppins pulling things out of her carpetbag of tricks. The only difference was that I was going to need more than a spoon full of sugar to help this next idea go down. "Now, before you say anything—"

"No way!" Liz shouted as soon as she saw what was in my hand. "No way. No how. Uh-uh."

I held out the flat iron to her. She looked at it like it was some kind of weapon of mass destruction. We'd been round and round about this forever. I'd wanted to straighten my hair for years, but never had the nerve to do it. Of course, Liz was never any help in that area.

"I would kill for tight curls like yours," she said for the umpteenth time since I first mentioned the idea back in junior high. "You hair's got style. *And* bounce."

"The first rule of getting the guy in these movies is to have a makeover," I said, grabbing an old VHS copy of *Clueless* off her bookshelf and the DVD of *The Princess Diaries* I rented as evidence. "It's Ro Com 101."

"Too bad you don't wear glasses," Liz joked. "I'd love to fit you for some contacts."

"Very funny."

Liz grabbed a handful of popcorn. "Fine," she said popping one piece in her mouth at a time as she spoke. "But we are not . . . using some piece . . . of junk you bought . . . at a mall kiosk. You are going to go to a licensed professional."

"Why?" I asked. "I've got the next best thing right here."

She rolled her eyes. "At least wait for Mom to get home." She was, of course, referring to the fact that her mom was an Emmy-winning and Oscar-nominated hairstylist and had a lot of experience in this area.

"You know your mom loves my hair more than you do," I said. "There's no way she'd let us do this."

"True." Liz seemed to be considering her options. Like she had any. If Liz didn't agree to help, she knew I'd only do it myself. And *that* never worked out for me. The one time I tried to color my own hair back in tenth grade I wound up with a crazy red fro that looked like a clown's wig. It was *not* pretty.

I took the long pause that followed as yet another good sign.

"Okay," Liz said, picking up Christy Caldwell's first film, *Room for Rent*. "But we're watching your new BFF's movie and making fun of her from beginning to end."

"Naturally," I said.

Liz took the flat iron out of the package and went over the instructions. Using her personal hair care products, she prepped my hair and then sat me front of the television. "One last chance to back out," she said.

I looked at my friend in the mirror beside the TV. I was actually getting nervous. Now that we were about to do the one thing I'd been talking about for years, I was afraid I was going to chicken out.

"Do it," I said.

I focused on the TV screen as Liz hit play. *Room for Rent* opened with a cute little animated credit sequence where a stick-thin version of a girl who was supposed to be Christy threw all her recently *ex*-boyfriend's clothing and stuff out their second floor window. As the credits rolled on, the items going out the window got crazier and bigger until the animated Christy shoved a full-grown elephant out. It hung in the air for a moment, then dropped and landed on the ex-boyfriend.

Cue the live action scene of Christy sitting alone in a half-empty apartment, crying.

While the sequence ran, Liz prepped my hair and got to work. "I'm going to start with a little piece," she said, separating a small curl from the forest on my head. I exhaled the breath I hadn't realized I'd been holding in and watched Liz's reflection in the mirror beside the TV, forgetting all about the movie.

She stretched out a piece of my hair and clamped down as the fold-out paper had instructed, slowly sliding the straightener down to the end of the hair.

"How's it look?" I asked, straining for a closer look in the mirror.

"Stop watching me and watch the movie," Liz cautioned. "And keep your head still."

I raised my hand in salute. "Yes, ma'am."

She tugged on my hair in response.

"I'm going to try a larger chunk of hair," she said, sounding skeptical, which was kind of typical for her.

I winced as she gathered up my curls. "Go ahead."

I focused on the movie again. We were getting to the part where Christy's best friend was giving her apartment a makeover that was heavy on leopard prints and purple shag carpeting.

Talk about tacky.

Still, it was a nice moment. Christy really sold the scene by playing it with a combination of vulnerability and strength. It was weird to think I'd spent the better part of the previous evening with the girl who was on-screen.

The burned popcorn smell had made it all the way upstairs now. It was not a pleasant smell. Hopefully it would clear out before Liz's parents got home.

The scene switched to an obligatory montage of Christy interviewing potential roommates, with each being worse than the last. It was difficult to enjoy with Liz tugging on my head.

"What are you doing?" I asked.

"Nothing," she squeaked in response.

My eyes went right to the mirror. I'd known Liz almost my entire life. She'd never squeaked like that before. In the reflection, I saw her struggling with the flat iron and a rather large chunk of my hair.

That was the point I realized it wasn't burned popcorn that I'd been smelling.

"Liz?"

She didn't respond, but she kept struggling.

I could see smoke starting to rise out of my curls.

"Liz?!"

"Hold on," she said through clenched teeth.

My head was getting hot. Really hot.

"LIZ!"

Six

I ran my hands through my painfully short hair and tried my hardest not to cry in front of the tourists. It was still in the same small curls I'd had since birth, but way shorter than it had ever been in my life. We're talking *Felicity* short, here. The damage was done less than twenty-four hours earlier and the wounds were still too fresh.

I tried not to be mad at Liz. It wasn't her fault that the flat iron I bought clamped down on my hair and refused to let go. Liz had done everything possible to get my hair free from the death grip that cheap piece of metal and plastic had on me while it fried my hair to a crisp. Finally she had managed to unplug the thing from the wall while my head continued to smolder.

I'm just glad I didn't go up in flames.

Liz had been forced to cut me free of the torture instrument. The little bit of hair that was left sprung right back into a curl. The flat iron went straight into the trash once it was cool. And I was left with a hole in my hair.

Liz did her best to cover up the hole with the hair around it, but there was only so much magic she could work. Even her mom couldn't manage it, and she was like a goddess when it came to hair.

The only option was to trim the rest of my hair down to match the part that had been burned off. And boy, did Liz's mom enjoy telling me what an *estúpido* idea it had been to try to straighten my hair in the first place. I can always tell how upset she is when she slips into Spanish.

I had to give her credit, though. You couldn't even tell that there was a patch in the back that was somewhere between curly and straight. I knew because I'd spent every free moment of the morning in the restroom, angling my compact behind my head to check my hair out in the mirror over the sink.

I tried to put my hair out of my mind and focus back on the tourists since we'd reached the Bric-a-brac Shack, signaling that the tour had come to an end. "And so ends our nearly one-hundred-year history of Sovereign Studios," I said. "Who knows what the future holds in store for us here at Sovereign? What new films will be produced? What lucky person will be plucked out of obscurity and turned into one of the most famous actors of all time? Who knows?" I repeated as I looked at each of my tourists. "Maybe it will be one of you."

Pause for dramatic effect.

Cheesy, I know, but the tourists eat it up.

"Hope you enjoyed the tour," I said. "Show your ticket at the register and you'll get a ten-percent discount on your purchases."

I said good-bye and they thanked me for the tour. No tips that morning, but I could tell they enjoyed it, which was good enough considering my mood. Since the tourists were at the store, my responsibility for them was officially over, so I headed out for lunch. I had an hour off until the second and final tour of the day.

En route to the commissary, I stopped at

the page break room to splash some water on my face and take another quick look at my hair. It looked exactly the same as it had every other time I'd seen it that morning. Now it was just a bit more plastered to my head from the heat. My plan to find movie love wasn't off to a good start, but I wasn't going to let a minor setback—okay, a major hair emergency—stop me. Connor had commented on my hair the other evening. Maybe he would like this even better.

Once I'd freshened up, I grabbed the lunch Mom had kindly packed for me that morning; leftovers from the dinner she had ordered from Dad's favorite restaurant to thank him for the flowers. After I nuked the orange chicken in the microwave, I joined Liz in the cafeteria. I found her at our usual table by the window with an extra frozen yogurt waiting for me. She must have really felt bad about my hair to spring for the treat.

As Liz had done, I pushed aside my lunch to indulge in dessert first. The cool strawberry yogurt hit the spot after the hot tour.

"So, Brillo," Liz said as I dug in. "We still working on Operation Ro Com or did the hair-tastrophe kill that idea?"

"Oh, I like that," I said as I reached into

my bag. "I hadn't come up with a name yet." I put my new notebook on the table between us and wrote "Operation Ro Com" at the top of the first page.

"Guess that answers my question." Liz grabbed the book and flipped through the pages. "Somebody's been busy."

"I was inspired," I replied while she skimmed my notes. We'd been so preoccupied by my hair drama the day before that we'd never had the chance to discuss what we had learned during our Ro Com marathon. Once Liz's mom got back from work, we'd been pretty much in hair crisis–control mode.

After I got home and my parents had their own freak-out about my hair over dinner, I went to my room to put together my plan. I'd been up till three o'clock in the morning watching the rest of the DVDs and writing down everything that came to mind.

I stole the book back from Liz. "Okay," I said, flipping to my summary. "To recap what we learned yesterday. Most romantic comedy films follow a certain formula."

"No kidding," Liz said with a snort. I don't know why she was being so negative about it. I caught her tearing up at the end of *Sleepless in Seattle*. I know she was totally into it.

"It usually starts with the heroine," I continued. "The female lead always has some character flaw," I explained. "She can be insecure, like Kirsten in *Bring It On*. Or have a short-term memory, like Drew in *50 First Dates*. Or be a total type A personality—"

"Ding, ding, ding!" Liz said, bouncing in her seat. "We have a winner."

"What are you talking about?"

"Your personality flaw."

I considered what my alleged friend was trying to imply. "Are you saying I'm anal?"

"Tracy, dear, you're sitting here plotting out your next romance like it's some film script, studying DVDs of movies that you want to emulate, and breaking them down in some crazy film analysis so you can apply them to life. If you don't think that's Type-A then you must be using the Greek alphabet."

"*Anyway*," I said, ignoring her insult. "A lot of the time the women in these movies are klutzes. Amanda Bynes can hardly take two steps without falling over something. Usually herself."

"That's because most romantic comedies are written by men who don't understand women enough to give them actual flaws that reflect the three-dimensional beings that we are," Liz said.

"And because watching people fall down is funny," I added.

"Exactly," Liz agreed with a bright smile.

"Once the leading characters are established," I continued, "they usually have what's called a 'meet cute.' I learned about that in *The Holiday*."

"Must have missed that one," Liz said. I didn't bother reminding her that I'd seen that movie on a date with a guy we eventually wound up nicknaming Dragon Breath for obvious reasons.

"A meet cute," I said, like I was teaching a class on this stuff, "is when they see each other for the first time in some awkward or endearing way. Like spilling a drink on someone or both people reaching for the same book and their hands touch."

"Aww," Liz said with a gag. "How adorable. But you've already met Connor."

"True," I said, "but knowing this stuff gives us something to work with."

"Then you'd better start working," Liz said. "Because the object of your affection just walked in."

Liz nodded toward the entrance, where I saw Connor coming in with one of his friends. The light blue oxford Connor was wearing hugged his torso quite nicely and looked great with his white pants. So few guys can pull off the white pants look, but Connor's skin tone was perfect for it.

Which just made me feel worse about the shapeless polyester uniform I was stuck in.

"So, what's your move?" Liz asked as we watched Connor get in line. "How would you script this scene?"

"Watch and learn," I said as I got up and moved toward the entrance to the serving area. Out of the corner of my eye I saw Liz practically running to the exit side of the partition so she wouldn't miss a thing.

I got more nervous as I crossed the commissary. I wasn't sure how Connor was going to react to seeing me. Christy Caldwell did slip right past him the other night before escaping the premiere. I can't imagine that his bosses were happy that he'd let her get away. Not that he really could have done anything about it. But still, it was possible that Connor might be upset with me for the part that I played in the whole thing.

I had to push all that from my mind. There was already enough to worry about making sure I did this right. Connor had been about to ask me out the other night. I was pretty sure of that. All I had to do was set up the situation where he could go through with what he'd intended.

I sauntered up to Connor. He had gotten out of line to hit the salad bar. I guess none of the pre-packaged stuff in the fridge looked good to him.

He was using the tongs to add an excessive amount of black olives to his salad. I took that as a good sign. I love black olives. But not as much as I loved the look on his face when he saw me coming his way. The smile seemed to suggest that he wasn't holding any grudge about the premiere. That was good.

Connor gave me a wave with the tongs. I waved back—with my hand.

I glanced past him to see Liz leaning around the partition to watch. She was smiling in anticipation like she was enjoying the show.

My eyes fell back to Connor, who looked even better the closer I got to him.

I took a deep breath. It was now or never.

It was time for our meet cute . . . even though we'd already met.

When I was only a few feet away from him I slipped my right foot in front of my left and tripped over myself. The move was subtle, yet fluid—exactly like I'd practiced it in my room a bunch of times before leaving for work. And I would have landed perfectly in his arms if only I had waited for him to put down his plate and the tongs.

I fell into Connor's chest harder than I'd expected, forcing the salad plate out of his hands and crashing to the floor—and calling everyone's attention in our direction.

I tried to reach out to hold onto something, *anything*, but my hands only grasped the air as my body tangled with Connor's and we both fell over.

Thankfully, the salad bar stopped our fall.

If only it hadn't been on wheels.

The bar slid out from behind Connor, slamming into the wall as we crashed to the floor. The entire commissary had gone quiet.

I could feel all eyes in the area on us. Liz

seemed both horrified for me and embarrassed to know me.

I looked up into Connor's confused face, trying to come up with a witty line to make fun of the uncomfortable situation. That's what would happen in a movie. The girl would say something funny. They'd share a cute laugh. He'd help her up and the meet cute would officially be a success.

I would have come up with a good line, too. If only the salad bar's sneeze guard hadn't come crashing down on our heads first.

Seven

My head was throbbing. That was one of the main differences between real life and the movies. In movies, klutzy people only hurt their pride. In real life, they hurt their pride, their head, both their elbows, and their butt. And that was only counting *my* injuries. I was afraid to ask what I'd hurt on Connor.

Not that I had the chance.

"Everyone, please clear a space," one of the studio's Emergency Medical Technicians said to the gathering crowd. He and another EMT pushed their way through the group as everyone parted for them. I could see Liz stuck in the back of the crowd, standing on tiptoe trying to determine if we were okay.

I tried to flash her a smile so she didn't worry, but I doubt she saw it over all the heads craning to gawk.

"I'm fine," I said to the lead EMT as he gently separated me from Connor. I swear, this studio must hire some of the hottest guys in town because the one tending to me was tall, dark, and oh-so-juicy. I made a mental note to introduce him to Liz later, since I was focused on Connor at the moment. Although I also thought it might be a good idea to keep the EMT in mind in case Connor never wanted to speak to me again considering I was turning out to be a bit of a jinx.

"It was a pretty bad crash," the EMT said. The name Craig was sewn into the dark blue uniform shirt that was straining against the muscles in his arms and torso. "We heard it from the other end of the cafeteria."

Just my luck that the EMTs would be at lunch when I made my bonehead move. Make that my *second* bonehead move, considering my hair fiasco. So far, Operation Ro Com was a total bust.

I tried to apologize to Connor, but the other EMT was busy quizzing him while Craig had a flashlight in my eye.

"Stop that," I said, smacking his hand

away. I did not have time for this. Connor probably thought I was a buffoon.

"I need to get you to the infirmary," Craig said. "Can you walk?"

I pushed him away. "Of course I can walk," I said, getting up a little too fast. The room lurched and I grabbed onto Craig's arm. "I'm okay," I said. And I was. Just not okay enough to stand so quickly.

Craig escorted me out of the cafeteria before I could say anything to Connor or Liz. Two electric carts, painted red to note their emergency vehicle status, sat beside the back door of the commissary. I'd seen the carts occasionally around the studio but I never imagined that I'd be riding in one. They looked like little trucks with a bench seat in the front and a small flatbed in the back where patients could lie if they were unconscious or whatever.

"You're not going to make me—"

"You can sit beside me," Craig said.

I thanked him as I got in the emergency cart and we took off. I was glad the thing didn't have lights and a siren. I'd already been embarrassed enough for one day. I didn't need the entire studio looking at me.

It only took a minute for us to reach the infirmary, where the EMT handed me off to the lone doctor before, I assume, going back to his lunch. Just as the emergency ride was a new experience, I'd never been in the infirmary before either.

Sovereign Studios is like a self-contained city in the middle of Hollywood. It has its our own little hospital, a miniature fire station and police station, a post office, hairdressers, a gym, and even a car wash. The studio executives are big on talking about how they take care of their employees. I think they just don't want anyone wasting time by going off the lot to run errands during the workday.

The "emergency room" was the size of my living room, containing a pair of exam tables and various glass cabinets filled with medical supplies. The doctor had me hop up on one of the exam tables as she pulled a privacy curtain, shutting us off from the rest of the room.

Like the EMT, the doctor also examined my eyes with a flashlight while asking me a series of questions. While she was checking my skull for damage, we both heard the front door open.

The doctor left my side, going around the curtain to tend to the new visitor. I figured that it was probably the other EMT with Connor, but I couldn't tell since the curtain blocked my view. I strained to listen to the voices of the EMT and the doctor, but I couldn't make out what they were saying. When I finally heard Connor's voice, I relaxed considerably—then panicked over what I was going to say to him once we could talk. My planned meet cute had been set for a conversation in the caf. Once emergency personnel had become involved, we'd veered disastrously away from the script. I wasn't sure how to play things with Connor at the moment. I wouldn't have been so worried, but I still had no idea how he was going to react to our mutual destruction.

The doctor returned to finish the examination way before I had my next course of action plotted out. She was quite attentive, double-checking everything she'd already checked. I suspect our accident was the most action she'd seen in a while. Working at the studio infirmary wasn't exactly like a real ER. Or even the one on television. There was always the risk of accidents while filming movies and TV shows, but I was pretty sure that most of the doctor's time was spent dispensing aspirin to the studio accountants after a movie had a poor opening weekend.

The doctor gave me the all-clear, but said she wanted me to stay and rest up a bit before my afternoon tour. She then pushed back my curtain and went across the room to check on Connor. His privacy curtain hadn't been pulled all the way closed, so I could see most of him while the doctor gave him the once-over. He didn't look all that bad from where I was sitting. Not bad at all.

Even battered and holding an ice pack to his head, Connor was still hot. His shirt was open and I could see that his great tan did not end at the bottom of his sleeves. Not surprising since we lived in Southern California, but still nice to look at.

And while I was looking, I made a mental note to see if I could get an ice pack to keep me cool on my afternoon tour.

As far as I could tell, Connor looked fine. Super fine, really, but I wasn't concentrating on his fine form at the moment. Well, not entirely. I was looking for any sign that I'd damaged him.

He appeared lucid, answering the doctor's

questions. He was far enough away that I couldn't make out exactly what he was saying, but his voice sounded strong. It was a relief when I heard him laughing with the doctor. I figured people with brain damage wouldn't laugh so genuinely like that, so he must be okay.

The doctor finally went to her office to record her notes. I took a deep breath, slipped off my table, and walked—carefully and without incident—over to Connor.

"Sorry," I said. "I'm not usually that big of a klutz."

"No, it was cool," Connor said. "I've never demolished a salad bar before. Now I can cross that off my list of things to do before I die."

Somehow, I doubted his list was real like Liz's.

I took the jokey tone of his voice to mean that he wasn't angry with me and relaxed a bit. Maybe Operation Ro Com still had a chance. "Do you have a long list of things you want to destroy?" I asked in a flirty kind of way. "And, more importantly, what have you already crossed off the list?"

"Oh, you know, the typical stuff," he said. "Dishes, cars . . . a few body parts. I broke my leg real good back in the fourth grade during an intense game of kill-the-guy-with-the-football. The bone was sticking through the skin and everything."

"Wow," I said, a bit grossed out. He did look adorable while reliving the memory, though. While I was apologizing, I figured it wouldn't hurt to get something else out of the way. "Sorry about the other night too. You didn't get in trouble for losing Christy Caldwell?"

"Not too bad," Connor said. "My boss says Christy does that kind of thing all the time. It wasn't that big a deal."

"So, you don't hate me?"

"How could I hate you?" he asked. "I hardly know enough about you to hate you."

"You could always learn more on Friday night," I suggested. If Connor had been caught even half as much by surprise as I was with my own boldness, he didn't show it. I'd asked guys out on dates before, but never so abruptly. I guess I wasn't thinking all that straight at the moment. It was possible that I had gotten a head injury from the accident. But it was far more likely that the sight of his bare chest peeking out from his open shirt was distracting me.

"Unless you already have plans," I said, giving him an out in case I had totally misread the situation and he wasn't that into me. I couldn't bring myself to look him in the eye while I waited for his response.

"As a matter of fact, I do have plans," Connor said. But before I could even try to mask my disappointment, he added, "I'm going out with a girl who literally fell into my arms."

"That's me, right?" I asked. I wasn't sure if that kind of thing happened to him often. You never know in Hollywood.

This evoked a smile from Connor. "Yes. That's you."

"Oh, okay, cool," I said, slightly stunned. I quickly looked around for a piece of paper or something to write my number on before he came to his senses and changed his mind. All my stuff was back at the commissary. I assumed that Liz had taken care of it for me, but I wasn't worried about any of that at the moment.

Finally, I found a pen sitting on the counter across the room. I grabbed it, but there was no paper. Not even a prescription notepad, though I doubt any doctor would leave those lying around. I was considering going through the drawers and cabinets, but I didn't think the doctor would have appreciated that. Besides, they were probably locked.

"Here," Connor said, ripping off a piece of the sanitary paper that was covering the exam table.

"Good thinking," I said as I took it from him. I wrote my cell number on the paper and handed it back. "Here."

"Great," he said as he took the pen and ripped another piece of paper, writing his own number down. "And one for you."

"Thanks." I nearly jumped as his hand reached up and ran through my incredibly short hair. His touch raised my temperature way hotter than it was outside. The move was about as sudden as my asking him out, but equally as welcome.

The pleasure quickly turned to embarrassment when I saw that his hand had come out of my hair with something in it.

"You had an olive in there," he said. "From the salad bar."

My face went a hundred different shades of red. "Oh." I tried to play it off. "I love olives."

"Me too," he said, and we both looked

down at the olive in his hand, which caused us both to laugh.

I said, "I don't."

"Yeah. No." He dropped the olive in the wastebasket beside us. Maybe in some cheesy bad movie someone would have found it all "meet cute" if he popped the olive that had been in my hair into his mouth, but I was pretty sure both of us thought that would have been disgusting.

After the olive was in the trash, we had a moment of awkwardness as we stood looking at each other trying to come up with something to say. This was now our third chance at conversation and we were still blowing it.

I guess Connor caught me staring, because he suddenly realized his chest was exposed and buttoned up his shirt.

He didn't look embarrassed about it though.

I checked my watch so it didn't look like I was watching him button up . . . because I totally was. My tour was supposed to start in ten minutes and I still had to find Liz to get my jacket. And the commissary was all the way on the other side of the lot. The distance only took a minute by emergency vehicle, but a bit longer on foot.

"I don't think either of you have permanent damage," the doctor said as she came back to us.

For some reason I felt like she had caught us in the middle of something, and I took a couple steps away from Connor.

"Just some bumps and bruises," she continued. "But maybe you want to stick to the pre-packaged salads for a while. To be on the safe side."

"Okay," we both said. Neither of us laughed at her lame joke.

"You're both fine to go," she said.

We thanked the doctor and made our way out of the infirmary. I stopped on the front steps, clearly wanting to say something. Anything. Connor stopped too, but he was just as quiet.

As we stood there about to go our separate ways, all I could think about was this part of my tour. The entire studio, from the offices to the paseo to the commissary, has been used for filming locations over the decades. Connor and I were standing in the exact spot where Rupert Charles and Delores Devore had their famous good-bye scene in the Sovereign Studios classic *Penny for Your Thoughts*.

"Um . . . well . . . bye," he said.

"Um . . . yeah . . . bye," I said.

Okay, not exactly a comparable good-bye scene to the classic, but we still had our date to get things right.

Eight

"I look like Princess Fiona," I said as I saw myself in the mirror, wearing a monstrosity. The green dress was lumpy and hung at odd angles that made me look very much like the female lead of *Shrek*.

"On the bright side, that part was played by Cameron Diaz," Liz said in an attempt to console me. It wasn't working.

The dress had looked so good on the hanger. Just not on my body. "Maybe Bloomingdale's was a bad idea," I said as I went back into the dressing room. It was the eighth dress I'd tried on, and each one had looked worse on me than the next.

"Told you we should have gone to the Galleria," Liz said.

"I am not getting a dress for my date at the Galleria," I said as I put my clothes back on. After work, we'd changed out of our uniforms to hit the Beverly Center. I needed the perfect outfit for Friday night. Since I was modeling my relationship on a movie plot, I figured I should look like a movie star on my first date. The high-end mall at the edge of Beverly Hills was where all the celebs shopped, so I knew that was where we had to go.

I left the dressing room, put the dress back on the rack, then grabbed Liz by the arm and left the department store. There was an entire mall at our disposal. No need to waste any more time than we already had in the overpriced department store.

The mall was pretty quiet for a Thursday evening, but it was still early. In my Old Navy jeans and Target T-shirt I felt woefully underdressed for the Beverly Center, where the average shopper was dressed up in a D&G suit or dressed down in Diesel jeans. There was no Sears in the Beverly Center. There was no JC Penney. Which is why I'd chosen it for my shopping trip. My paycheck had already been direct-deposited and I could think of nothing better to spend it on, although I'm sure that my parents could have come up with a few ideas.

Liz and I spent the next hour and a half going in and out of Club Monaco, bebe, and Planet Funk in search of the perfect outfit. I tried on classic dresses, modern skirts, and vintage jeans and T's. Nothing was working for me. The few things that did look good cost more than my paycheck, so I had some real trouble justifying the purchases. I wanted to *look* like a movie star, not *spend* like one.

We were going to take a break and stroll through Restoration Hardware when I saw a new boutique. It didn't look to be part of the typical expensive chain stores. In fact, it didn't even have a name above the door, just a blue neon dress. But it did have some fabulous dresses in the window.

I pulled Liz into the store and found the most perfect of perfect dresses on my first try. It had a silky, blue-gray, camisole-type top with spaghetti straps that draped down into a pencil skirt. Very forties modern. One part Katharine Hepburn and one part Katherine Heigl, it was casual for a night hanging out at the movies, but formal enough for a nice dinner. The design would go perfectly with my new hairstyle. Grabbing a dress in my size, I hurried into the dressing room to try it on.

Wow! was all I could think when I saw my reflection. I had never looked so good in my entire life, if I do say so myself. It was the perfect dress.

And it only took me two hours to find.

"How's it look?" Liz asked from outside the dressing room.

"See for yourself," I said as I slid the curtain back in a fluid move that unveiled me wearing the most perfect dress in the universe.

"Wow," Liz said.

"My thoughts exactly," I said, giving a little spin.

"How much?" she asked.

"I don't know," I said, pointing to the tag hanging out of the back of the camisole. "All that's there is some inventory code."

"Trace," she said in a tone that always preceded doom as she grabbed the tag. "That's not an inventory code. That *is* the price."

"No!" I said, reaching behind my back for the tag. There was no way I could see it behind me, but I remembered most of the number. It was way more digits than a price tag should have. Certainly more than my next *three* paychecks would cover. The perfect dress could not possibly be that far out of my price range. That would go against the entire definition of "perfect."

"Excuse me," Liz flagged down the nearest saleslady. I felt a gentle tug on my back as Liz held out the tag. "Is this the price?"

"Yes," the saleslady said. "But we are having a sale."

Even at a half-off sale the price would have demolished my college fund. It was the most expensive dress I'd ever had on my body. The thing cost like ten times more than my prom dress. Still, I held my breath as she told us the markdown.

"Everything in this section is ten percent off," she said in the most annoyingly chipper way.

"Thanks," Liz said as she sent the saleslady along with a wave. "Well, at least you got to see yourself in it."

"It *is* on sale," I said.

"Ten percent barely covers the tax," she reminded me. It was only a slight exaggeration. "Take it off."

I stole another glance in the mirror. "I will."

The dress hung perfectly on my frame. It accented my hips and minimized my butt. It fixed every flaw and highlighted every asset on my body. I guess that's why they could charge so much for it.

"Tracy," Liz said in a warning tone. It was like she knew what I was thinking. "You can't buy that dress."

Okay, so she actually *did* know what I was thinking.

I pulled her closer to me. "Hear me out," I whispered, making sure the saleslady was not within earshot. Conveniently, she was helping a couple of Beverly Hills trophy wives on the other side of the store. "I know I can't afford this, but that doesn't mean I can't buy it."

"Yes. Yes it does. That's exactly what it means."

"No, listen," I insisted. "It's only expensive if I keep it. I can buy it tonight on my credit card, wear it on my date tomorrow, and return it Saturday. I'll get the credit back on the card before my parents even realize the money was spent."

"When did you switch from a movie script to TV?" Liz asked. "That's like the oldest plot element in sitcom history. Some obsessed character buys an outfit she can't afford. She has every intention of returning it. But then she spills some coffee down the front, or finds a sweaty handprint on the back, or gets the bottom caught in a paper shredder. And then she's stuck having to pay for it. No, Trace. No matter how hot you look in that dress, it's not worth it."

"You think I look hot?"

Liz rolled her eyes. "That was *so* not the moral of the story."

I took a deep breath. "I'm getting it."

Liz knew me well enough to know there was no arguing with me at this point. She just put her head in her hand, shaking it in resignation.

I carefully got out of the dress and hung it on the hanger, then got back into my regular clothes. I was really glad that I'd changed after work. If my body had had to get back into my uniform after wearing that dress, my skin would have broken out in hives of revolt. I was having enough trouble adjusting to the natural cotton fibers I was wearing.

I could tell Liz was still angry when I came out of the dressing room. It was nice that she cared so much, but honestly, it wasn't her money. Technically, it wasn't my money either since I was still on my parents' credit cards, but if everything worked out, they wouldn't know about it—at least, not for a while.

Liz followed me up to the register. She was so busy glaring at me that we didn't say anything until the transaction was over. I did have a moment of hesitation when the saleslady asked for my credit card. But then I remembered how I looked in the dress and handed it over with a smile that matched hers.

Once the dress was bought, Liz gave up on her argument entirely. She checked her watch as we left the store. "Dex should be done with his callback. He's probably waiting for us at CPK."

"Then let's go get some dinner," I said with a bright smile. I didn't care if my best friend thought I was an idiot. I was an idiot who was going to look good on her date Friday night.

We rode the Beverly Center's escalators down from the mall and past the parking structure beneath it to the California Pizza Kitchen that was on street level. CPK was packed as usual, but we only had to wait a few minutes for a seat. Dex had already gotten there and put his name in.

The hostess sat us at a table by the window where we looked over the menus in total silence. We even ordered without commenting on one another's selections, which is so unlike us. I wanted to ask about Dex's callback for the play he'd auditioned for, but I knew better. If he wasn't saying anything about it, there was nothing yet to say. So the three of us sat in silence for what felt like hours.

It wasn't a surprise that Dex sensed something was up. "Am I missing something?" he asked as the waiter brought us our bread.

"Nothing," I said. I wasn't about to get into the whole dress thing again. But I did want to tell Dex about my date with Connor, because I was going to need his help with the next phase of my plan. I just wasn't sure where to begin.

"I'm kind of in the middle of this thing," I said, grabbing a piece of bread. "It's sort of like a . . ." I was having trouble finding the right word. It certainly wasn't a game, but calling it a scheme just sounded wrong.

"You mean Operation Ro Com?" Dex asked. "Liz told me all about it."

I turned in the direction of my supposed best friend. She shoved an entire piece of bread in her mouth and turned away from me, focusing on the people on the street so I could not kill her with my glare. I threw a hand up, giving her a "whatever" gesture. Truth be told, she saved me from having to explain it all to Dex. "And you get what I'm doing?"

"I don't know what you see in Intern Guy—"

"His name is Connor."

"—but it's your life."

"Good," I said. "Because I need your help."

"This should be fun," Liz said. Her eyes were still locked on the street.

"I need to find something crazy romantic to do on this date. Something memorable. Something that would be out of a scene from a movie."

"You could hack up your date with a machete," Dex suggested.

"Wrong movie," I said.

"Why don't you let Connor decide where he wants to take you?" Liz suggested, coming back into the conversation.

"I'm going to," I said. "I'm not completely controlling. If this thing's going to work out between us, he's got to contribute too. I'm just looking for some insurance that our first date will be truly remarkable. And story worthy. You guys read *True Love*. You've heard all about my parents' romance. You know what I have to live up to."

"You don't have to live up to anything," Dex said. "You just have to be yourself."

That made me laugh. "Easy for you to say. You're like the most romantic person I've ever met."

"You need to get out more," Liz said, pulling apart another piece of bread.

"Be serious," I said. "You know he is. Like that time he sent Psycho Loser on that scavenger hunt where she had a rose at every destination and he was waiting for her at the end with a candlelit dinner that she never touched."

"Because his choice of meal wasn't on her diet," Liz added.

"Hey!" he said.

"Or on Psycho Loser's birthday, when he took her to the beach and read her classic love poems," Liz added.

"And all she could do was complain that he didn't buy her a gift?" I finished the thought. "I miss Psycho Loser. She was so much fun to make fun of."

"Can we please not mention my ex by name?" Dex asked.

"Sorry," we said. We'd thought he was finally over her. Dex and Psycho Loser had been dating all through high school. Liz and I suspected that she'd been cheating on him the entire time, but we'd never been able to find any proof.

Dex had treated that girl like she was a queen and she never even thanked him for it. He did the kind of stuff that people really did write movies about and she just expected it. And the worst part was that she broke up with him the morning after Valentine's Day, senior year. Liz and I suspect that she'd made the decision to end it weeks earlier, but she'd wanted to milk one more holiday out of him before she dumped him.

Dex had only recently started dating again. So far, Liz and I hadn't been impressed with his choice of dates, but he was working through the transition. On the bright side, the pain he'd suffered from Psycho Loser had totally helped him in his acting. He did great as Stanley from *A Streetcar Named Desire* in the school show.

"So, what do you say?" I asked. "Will you help me?"

Dex took a bite of his bread. He tried to look like he was considering my request, but he was just stalling so I would beg.

"Pleeeeease," I pleaded. "I need that moment."

"What moment?" he asked.

"The moment in every movie where you know, without a question, that the girl and the guy have just fallen in love," I said. I quickly held up a hand when I saw Liz's mouth open. "I'm not talking about manufacturing any feelings for anyone," I clarified. "I mean real love. But if I can help push it along by creating that perfect moment, then all the better." If only I had any idea what that perfect moment could be. Since I didn't, I looked to an expert.

"Well," Dex said, "There is this one thing."

"Yes?"

"But I was kind of hoping to use it myself someday," he said.

"You still can," I said. I threw my right hand up in the air and put my left hand on the table like I was swearing on a bible. "I promise not to tell any girl you go out with in the future what you planned for me so that she will be surprised when you do the same thing for her."

Dex still looked hesitant. I could understand him not wanting to give away his best material, so I didn't want to pressure him. I waited silently for him to make the decision that we all knew he was going to make. . . . Okay, I may have given him my sad face too, but I couldn't help it if my expression reflected the way I was feeling. I wanted to hurry that decision along.

"Fine," he said. "I'll do it."

"Great!" I said, clapping my hands together in excitement. "Tell us about it."

"Oh no, Trace. This one is going to be a surprise."

"Bro, you can't. I need to know how to prepare."

"Sorry," he said as our food arrived. "You're going to be as much in the dark as the poor schmuck you're planning all this for." He pulled a piece of pizza off his plate before it even touched the table and shoved it in his mouth. It was his way of telling me that he was done talking about the subject.

I had total faith in Dex that he would plan something spectacular. I just wanted to know what it was. But I wasn't going to let him think that I was all dying to hear what he had in mind. To show him that I could play his game, I picked up my own slice of pizza and bit into it in the same haughty way he'd bitten into his.

I only wish I had let the slice cool down first, because it totally scorched the roof of my mouth.

Nine

"This is not a good idea," Liz said from her desk while she painted purple stars on a black skydiving helmet. Her skydiving birthday was not until the end of August, but she was doing everything possible to be ready for the event. Personally, I was still hoping she'd change her mind and let me throw her a big bash like she'd thrown for me on my eighteenth back when school ended. But Liz has hated parties ever since she was a kid. I think it has to do with her having to share every party with her twin brother. I still wasn't sure what Dex wanted to do to celebrate the milestone, but I was fairly certain he wasn't going to ask me to face death with him like his sister had tried to do.

"Enough with the negativity!" I said as I checked myself out in her mirror one more time. I had told Connor to meet me at her house so I didn't have to go through the awkward "meet my parents" routine. It was way too early in this possible relationship for me to have to deal with that. Not that my parents were harsh. It was just a lot of pressure.

Also, I didn't want my parents to see me in a dress that they weren't ever going to see again. It could lead to uncomfortable questions that I'd much rather avoid.

Speaking of the dress. "How does it look?" I asked.

"Like a million bucks," Liz said. "Which is half the price you paid for it."

"Stop being so dramatic."

"Stop scratching."

"I can't help it," I said as I rubbed the back of my neck. "The tag itches."

"Hmph," she said as she started another star. She was going to be the best dressed skydiver in her class, if I didn't kill her before I left for my date.

There was a loud bang on the door.

"Go away!" Liz yelled.

The door swung open and Dex flew into the room. "I got the pa—"

He froze mid-yell when he saw me. Since he'd seen me in Liz's room thousands of times over the years, I had to think that it was the dress that had stopped him in his tracks. "Wow. That's even better than you looked on prom night."

"Thank you," I said. Since Dex had still been reeling from his breakup three months earlier, I'd asked him to go to the prom with me as friends. That way, he didn't have to miss it, and I didn't have to spend the night with some random guy who just wanted to get me out of my dress.

I was going to ask him what he was so excited about when the doorbell rang, causing me to lose my mind. I turned to Liz and squealed, "It's Connor!"

"He's picking you up here?" Dex asked.

"I needed help with my prep," I said as I messed with my hair in the mirror. There wasn't much I could do with it, and it didn't seem to be laying right. "Dex, could you get that while we finish up?"

Liz sprung off her bed. "I got it."

"I need your help," I said.

"You're fine," Liz said as she went for the hall. "Besides, he won't be looking at anything but the dress."

"But—"

"Do you want my dad to get the door before I do?" Liz asked.

"Somebody go!" I said, waving my hands frantically. The last thing I wanted was Liz's dad to meet Connor. He could be worse than my own dad with the inquisition.

Once Liz was gone, I turned back to the mirror and played around with my hair some more. I wasn't really doing anything with it, but the mussing helped work off some of my nervous energy. I don't know why I was so anxious. I'd had plenty of experience going on first dates before. Then again, I was kind of putting a lot of pressure on this becoming more than just another first date.

"You already look great," Dex said. "You can stop with the fussing."

"Thanks," I said. "I'm nervous."

"That's because you're making this into too big a thing," Dex said, taking a seat on his sister's bed. "You've got plenty of time to have a serious relationship. Go out and have fun and see what happens."

I took a deep breath. Dex was right. I'd done all I could. Now it was up to the stars to align and the date to be whatever it was going to be. Once I calmed down, I remembered that Dex had come bouncing into the room for some reason, so I asked him what was up.

"I got the part!" he said, continuing the yell he had started when he entered.

I ran over to hug him, but stopped myself when I realized a tight squeeze would wrinkle the dress. He seemed to understand, and we awkwardly pounded fists before cracking ourselves up over how silly we must have looked.

"What's the play about?" I asked.

"It's a modern re-re-retelling of *Romeo and Juliet* called *RoJu*."

I tried not to let the horror of hearing that awful title show on my face.

"The script is terrible," he admitted. "But the director's brother is a casting agent for TV and he's coming opening night. I plan to impress him with my ability to overcome even the worst material."

"As I know you can," I said.

"Tracy!" Liz yelled from downstairs.

That was classy. I didn't bother to yell back.

"You've got everything set, right?" I asked as I moved to the bedroom door.

"Just text me when you get to the studio."

"And you still don't want to tell me what you put together for me and Connor?"

"I don't want to ruin the surprise," he said.

I gave him a twirl. "I really look okay?"

"Now you're just digging for compliments," Dex said. "You look great."

"Thanks," I said. "You look pretty good yourself." He was dressed in vintage from head to toe. Old jeans, a classic T-shirt, and a worn blazer he bought in a thrift store a few months ago. These were not sit-at-home-on-Friday-night clothes.

"I'm going out with a girl I met at auditions," he explained as he rifled through Liz's closet.

"Dating a costar?" I asked. "That's a bad idea."

"It's okay. She didn't get cast." He was still rifling through his sister's things, which I knew she wouldn't like. "You should take something to wear on top of that. It's going to get chilly tonight."

That's the crazy thing about Los Angeles. No matter how hot it is during the day, it's always cool at night.

I was worried about covering up my

dress. I'd sort of paid a lot of money to look as good as I did in it. I didn't want to ruin the effect for the sake of comfort. But when he pulled Liz's purple shawl out of the closet and I saw that it went perfectly with my outfit I took it as another sign that the dress was meant to be.

"Thanks," I said as he wrapped the shawl around my shoulders. "I can always count on you to take care of me." I gave him a quick kiss on the cheek and left to meet my date.

When I got to the top of the steps I realized that I was practically running. I stopped myself at the railing, took a breath, and slowly walked down the stairs. The last thing I needed was to trip in my excitement and go rolling down to Connor's feet though that would have fit in with the klutz character that Connor had already met.

Although they may not have even noticed. Connor had lifted up his pant leg and was pointing to something on his shin. "Sixteen stitches," he said. "Football injury."

"That's nothing," Liz said as she lifted her own pant leg. "Twenty stitches. Skateboarding accident."

I guess Connor saw me coming, because he leaned over and pointed to his head. "No stitches. Attacked by a salad bar."

"Very funny," I said as I joined them.

"Hey!" Connor said like he just noticed I was there. "You look nice."

"Thanks," I said. It wasn't quite the "Wow" I was hoping for, but I did like the way he was checking me out.

I gave him a gentle hug hello while I checked him out as well. As expected, he looked mighty fine, wearing black pants and a gray polo. His outfit totally worked with mine. I tried not to see it as a sign that we were meant for each other.

"Why didn't you tell me you're taking skydiving lessons?" he asked me.

My eyes unintentionally rolled. "I'm not," I clarified. "She is. I'm just going to wait on the ground freaked out of my mind until she lands."

"That would have been an awesome first date," Connor said.

He *had* to be kidding. As far as I was concerned, skydiving would have been a horrible first, second, third, or whatever date. Maybe as a fiftieth anniversary date, when we'd both lived a full life and were ready to die. But I still had a lot of things I wanted to do with my life before possibly plunging to my death.

"Now you two kids go and have fun," Liz said as she pushed us through the doorway. She raised an eyebrow when she laid her hand down on top of her own shawl, but she didn't say anything about it. We always borrowed each other's clothes so it wasn't a big deal. "And don't you keep her out too late, now."

"I won't, ma'am," Connor said with a laugh.

"And you be a gentleman," Liz said. "Or there will be hell to pay."

"Yes, ma'am," he said, giving her a salute.

We were laughing as we strolled to his car.

Connor spent the first half of the ride to the restaurant going on and on about how cool it was that Liz was planning to skydive. Apparently he'd always wanted to go skydiving. He said that maybe we could go skydiving some day. I was noncommittal on all counts, but getting quite tired of hearing the word "skydiving."

Eventually he exhausted that subject. Since he had a great mix playing on his iPod, I focused on that and we fell into a comfortable silence as we both hummed along the rest of the way. He wouldn't tell me where we were going for dinner, but I figured it out a block before we pulled into the overcrowded parking lot.

El Coyote Café is this crazy Mexican restaurant that's equal parts tourist trap and hip L.A. eatery. The food's okay, but the ambiance is really what you go for. There are tacky Mexican-type decorations on the walls, the waitresses all wear these huge Spanish dresses, and it's got this great link to an old Hollywood murder. What more could you ask for in a dining experience?

I was worried when I saw all the people sitting outside, waiting to get in. The place was always packed, so I expected a bit of a wait. I just wasn't sure if whatever Dex had planned was time-sensitive.

Connor pulled me along as he got in line to leave our name with the host. When it was our turn, I couldn't hear what he was saying, so I was caught entirely off guard when the host was suddenly leading us into the restaurant.

"But they don't take reservations," I said as Connor guided me along after the host.

"They do if you know how to make

them," Connor said cryptically. I suspect he called ahead using some studio bigwig's name. Maybe some money even changed hands. Either way, I was suitably impressed.

After spending a few minutes with Connor taking in the crazy atmosphere, I finally settled into the date and relaxed. We chatted a bit, ordered our food, and enjoyed each other's company. The date was going well, so far. And my dress was holding up *very* well, except for the tag that was jabbing into my back every time I leaned against the cushion. Maybe this Operation Ro Com was going to work after all.

"Try some of the salsa," Connor said. "It's great."

"I'm fine," I said with a shake of my head. There was no way I was going to risk a salsa spill even though I had a napkin on top of Liz's shawl in my lap. She would kill me if I spilled anything on her shawl, but it was replaceable. I knew exactly where in Target I could get her a new one since I was there with her when she bought the one I had with me.

"No, really. You have to." He took a tortilla chip from the bowl and dipped it into the hot salsa, lifting a generous amount into the air. A drip fell beside the salsa bowl as he held it out to me. "Just try it."

My eyes went wide as the dripping chip came closer. I leaned in as far as I could, with my chest hovering inches over the table, and quickly snapped the whole chip into my mouth in one bite. I was careful to remain in position until I had chewed it all and wiped any remains from the sides of my mouth.

Then I realized my mistake.

"It's *hot*!" I said, grabbing for my glass of water and swallowing half of it in one gulp. I'd wanted to order a virgin colada, but had opted for something with less stain possibilities.

"I didn't expect you to take it all in one giant bite!" Connor said with a laugh. "That was awesome!"

"Thanks," I said, glad that I had impressed him with my gluttonous ways.

I performed a subtle dress check. Nothing had dropped on it. That was good.

We lapsed into another silence. I think part of the reason for the lulls in conversation was that I was still trying to figure out what kind of character I wanted to play to ensure that the date developed into something more.

The klutz thing had worked in obtaining the date, but a spill on the dress would mean financial doom for me, so that was out. There were several romantic comedy archetypes that came to mind, but I wasn't sure if Connor was interested in shy and uncertain, outgoing and bold, or bitter and cold.

Probably not that last one. . . . And I wasn't about to try for Hooker with a Heart of Gold.

I decided on neutral and let Connor guide the conversation. That turned out to be one of the less successful parts of my plan when we hit yet another lull and Connor decided to fill it without me.

"Do you mind if I . . . ?" Connor waved his cell phone. I wasn't sure if he meant he wanted to call someone or what. And truthfully, I did mind. I like cell phones for their convenience, but am way sick of people who can't put it down at dinner. In keeping with my neutral character, I simply shrugged and let Connor read my response any way he saw fit.

"Thanks!" He flipped open the screen and started pushing buttons. On my list, people who text during dinner are even ruder than people who talk. If he had been talking to someone, at least I could have listened in on the conversation. As it was, all I could do was sit there and munch on tortilla chips—sans salsa.

"Yes!" Connor whooped as he flipped the screen shut. "Early estimates show that *Table for Two* is tracking well in the box office. It could be on its way to a fifty mil opening weekend."

"Wow," I said. Good for Christy. *Table for Two* was never going to be a huge summer blockbuster that topped a hundred million in one weekend. Those were usually action pics made from comic books, like *Spider-man*. Even half that for a romantic comedy would be record-breaking. But why did Connor need to know right then and there how the film was tracking? "Do you need to report that to someone?"

"No," Connor said. "Just curious. Don't you track movie openings?"

I shrugged. "Not really." I'm not so naive that I ignore the numbers completely. I do work in Hollywood, after all. But I can usually wait until the top ten list comes out on Sunday like most of the rest of the world. How much a movie makes isn't nearly as important as how good it is to me.

"Did you see it yet?" Connor asked.

"Not yet," I replied. I'd been so busy watching romantic comedies on DVD that I hadn't had the chance to see the movie that had inspired my plan. Besides, I'd kind of overdone it on Christy Caldwell movies in the past week. There's only so many perfectly happy endings a girl can take.

"We're poised to be the top-grossing romantic comedy of all time," Connor added. "We're already talking sequel. I know sequels usually suck, but we're trying to get back the original team. . . ."

What's with the "we"? I thought as Connor rambled on. I doubted that a marketing intern was in any of the high-level meetings where this kind of thing was discussed. And it wasn't like he had to impress me. I knew what his job was and already thought it was pretty cool considering he was only a year older than me.

As he went on about the marketability of a sequel, the waitress returned to our table with a precariously balanced tray of food in her hand. I slid as far in toward the wall as I could go as the waitress served us our meal.

"One chicken enchilada, extra cheese

and extra guacamole," she said as she placed a plate overflowing with various sauces in front of Connor. "And one salad. Extra olives. No dressing."

"Thank you," I said as she put my dinner in front of me. Honestly, I didn't feel the least bit appreciative of the rabbit food she'd put down, even though it was exactly what I'd ordered. It was the only thing on the menu with no stain potential—I even asked them to hold the tomatoes. If only it wasn't so bland.

"Something more to drink?" the waitress asked.

"Another virgin colada," Connor said through a mouthful of his meal.

"I'm fine," I said, holding up my half-empty glass of water.

The waitress looked at me like I was some pathetic wannabe starlet starving myself in the hope of getting my first acting gig. They probably got that a lot around there. I know I probably looked the part, nibbling on my salad and carefully sipping my drink to avoid water stains, but believe me, I can pack away a meal if I want to. Dex and I can eat Liz under the table when we go out for dim sum.

I regretted not having a snack before I went out to dinner.

"Man, you've got to try this," Connor said as he loaded up a heaping forkful of meat, cheese, sauce, and even more sauce.

"That's okay!" I quickly said before the gooey mess could make its way over to my side of the table.

"Really?" Connor examined his food hungrily as it hovered midway between us. "You don't know what you're missing."

I looked down at my dress again. I couldn't see the tag, but the credit card receipt was burned into my mind. "Oh, I do know," I said. "I certainly do."

I munched on my dry salad while Connor went on and on about his meal. It did look so very good. I soothed my pangs of jealousy by resolving to come back to the restaurant with him on a future date in an outfit more appropriate to Mexican dining. As much as I wished that I could have had more fun in the moment, I had bigger goals in mind than a simple first date.

Besides, I'd have the chance to enjoy myself once we moved on to the studio part of our evening. At least, that was my hope.

Ten

While Connor handed our ID cards to the security guard at the front entrance to the studio, I sent a quick text message to Dex saying, "We're here." By the time we were waved through the gate and Connor pulled into a spot in the main parking lot, I'd gotten my answer.

It said, "Stage 5."

I had no clue what Dex had in store for us there, but I knew it would be good. So far, the date was pretty okay. But we still needed that moment—that one-of-a-kind event that cinched it for us. And I was sure that Dex wouldn't let me down.

"Where are we going?" Connor asked as we got out of the car.

"It's a surprise," I said as he took my arm and I started walking toward Stage 5. Little did he know that it was a surprise for the both of us. I was getting excited as well, but as we got closer to Stage 5, that excitement turned to panic.

What if Dex's idea of romance turned out to be a dud? Or worse, what if he decided to play a trick on me and do something he thought was funny that would be horribly awful? Or even worse, what if it *was* the perfect moment and Connor hated every second of it?

Why couldn't Dex tell me what he was going to do? I wondered. My panicked mind starting coming up with alternate ideas—places we could go around the lot to have our moment. That spot on the roof at the New York backlot could certainly be romantic under the right circumstances.

I did my best not to let the panic show. Connor had seemed pretty willing to go to our mystery destination so far. He didn't seem the type to run off when something odd happened. Quite the opposite, actually.

Besides, Dex would never pull a prank on me that could sabotage my evening. He knew how much I had riding on this date.

And as for romance, there was nobody like him. I pushed the panic from my mind and clung tighter to Connor as we walked through the dimly lit studio.

It was relatively silent on the Sovereign Studios lot. Even though it was late on a Friday, we weren't the only people there, of course. Between production crews, the housekeeping staff, and power-hungry executives working into the wee hours of the morning, the Sovereign Studios lot was never empty. So when an electric cart with one headlight out carrying a giant fiberglass alligator passed us, I barely gave it a second glance.

"We're here," I said as we reached our destination.

Connor looked up at the huge number painted on the even larger building. "Stage Five?"

"This is where they filmed the cult classic *On Angel's Wings*," I told him as I opened the stage door and braced myself for whatever was waiting for us.

"Never saw it," Connor said. That wasn't a big surprise. Cheesy eighties movie musicals didn't exactly seem to be his type of entertainment as far as I could tell.

"You didn't miss much," I said as I peeked into the darkened stage.

I double-checked my phone to confirm we were in the right place. The screen still said "Stage 5." "Follow me," I said as I carefully entered the blackness of the unlit soundstage.

"I've never snuck onto a set before," Connor said in a whisper. "What's filming in here? Some top-secret movie that the studio doesn't want anyone knowing about yet?"

I loved the way his eyes were all squinty when he got excited. I could still see him from the outside light, but that would change once the door shut.

"No," I replied. "It's not a movie. It something much more"—I searched for the right word to describe something I had no clue about—"interesting."

The door closed behind us, punctuating my statement and shutting out all the light. I had another brief flash of panic that had more to do with anticipation than with the darkness surrounding us.

The soundstage was pitch-black, except for the small patch of light in the center of the cavernous room. I couldn't see if any dangers stood between the light and us, but

I trusted that Dex would have left me a clear path. When I looked down, I saw that he had. A line of two-inch-long patches of glowing tape ran right up to the spot of light.

Connor leaned in and whispered. "This is . . ." Like I'd done a moment ago, he was struggling to find the right word. I wasn't sure if the word he was looking for was "cool" or "fun" or "the most stupidly ridiculous date I've ever been on," but I was hoping for the best.

"Stay with me," I said. I didn't just mean I wanted him close by. I was beginning to worry that he was going to think I was some kind of freak and storm off. I mean, I was taking him into some dark soundstage to do who knew what. If something didn't happen soon, he might get weirded out by the whole thing and leave.

I carefully stepped into the darkness, following the path of tiny glowing squares on the floor. A few steps into the room, I felt Connor's hand reaching for mine. I really appreciated the darkness around me as I took his hand because my face burned bright red and a stupid grin stretched across my cheeks when we touched. It was embarrassing enough knowing he couldn't see it. I couldn't imagine how I would have felt if he had.

I could sense his nervous anticipation through his touch. But I doubt he was even half as excited as I was to have our perfect movie moment. If everything went the way I'd hoped, it was possible that Connor and I would soon be sharing the most romantic kiss that soundstage had ever seen! It had already experienced some historic embraces over the decades, but this one would be way better, because it was happening to me.

Though it was also possible that I was getting ahead of myself.

"We're here," Connor said in a soft whisper.

I clung to his hand. "We *so* are."

The tiny light that Dex had left for us was sitting on some kind of control board in front of me. It was a jumble of buttons and levels that I didn't have a clue how to figure out, with heavy wires leading out of the back and into the darkness. Thankfully, Dex had taken my mechanical shortcomings into consideration. A sticky note was on top of a green button on the console.

It said, "Press me."

I did as instructed.

A blue light slowly filled the darkness.

"Tracy, what's—"

I held up a hand. "Just wait."

I waited too. I should have expected that a lighting apprentice would have a light show planned when he instructed me to walk into a totally dark room. My excitement grew tenfold as the light shifted from blue to red and was joined by other lights, dancing in the darkness.

A foggy mist rolled in across the floor as the soundstage was lit. Even though the stage was bare, it was still exciting to look at the colored lights swirling around us. It was almost like they were telling a story, with the bolder colors chasing the softer ones around the stage. They would run up to one another and stop, then reverse directions in almost a playful way.

Connor's head craned in every direction as he watched the light show unfold. "How did you . . ."

"Movie magic," I replied, in awe myself. Truthfully, it had been Dex magic. I didn't want to spoil the moment by talking about another guy, no matter how amazing he'd been to set up this whole light show for me in one afternoon. I owed him big time.

All thoughts of Dex flew out of my mind as Connor wrapped his arm around my shoulder and pulled me closer to him. My heart was beating as fast as the flashing lights. To be so close to Connor. To be in his arms. It was exactly what I'd wanted.

The show grew into a frenzied storm of lights battling all around us. It was intense and passionate and forced me to cling tightly to Connor in the excitement. And the best part was, he totally clung back. We were both in the moment together. I could tell.

But then it stopped.

All the riotous dancing lights went dark, and the soft blue light that had started it all filled the air. But it wasn't alone. Music played from unseen speakers. I didn't recognize the tune, but it perfectly matched the blue light surrounding us. It wasn't a sad blue, like you'd normally associate with the color. It was a bright and happy blue, like the sky on a perfect day. And the song was bright and happy, but also sweet and romantic.

It was clear to me what we were supposed to do.

I stepped out of Connor's embrace, slipping his hand back into mine. "Dance with me," I said.

Suddenly, the confused look on Connor's face wasn't as cute as it had been earlier.

"Umm . . . I don't dance."

I froze. That was not in the script.

"But I can give it a try," he said with a shrug.

I ignored the uncertainty in his voice and plunged ahead with the dancing.

As much as I wanted to turn this into some kind of musical number from *Singin' in the Rain*, I figured it was best to keep it simple. I wrapped my arms around him and, keeping a respectable, but not too distant distance, I began to sway to the music, pulling him along with me.

The fog at our feet swirled around us as we moved. The lights started dancing along with us too, slowly weaving in and out of one another along with the music.

Once we got the basic rhythm down, I was hoping that the music would inspire Connor to take over and sweep me off my feet. Unfortunately, the sweeping was not exactly happening.

Connor couldn't even manage to find the beat. Not only was his swaying off tempo, it was at varying speeds. I tried to force him to move with me, but he wasn't exactly receptive to my less-than-gentle persuasion. When the dancing began to resemble a wrestling match, I gave up and let him lead.

It wasn't pretty—and I was starting to get a little seasick—but it felt nice to be in Connor's slim-but-nicely-toned arms. I eventually managed to block out everything but the music as I let my imagination create what Connor's moves could not. The date was finally on its way to absolute perfection.

We were going to have our moment. We were going to share our first kiss.

"What's going on in here?" a voice called out, snapping me back into reality.

I twisted my body toward the door to see who it was. At the same time Connor continued his jerky move to the side, which sent us tumbling to the concrete stage floor.

For the second time in a week, I landed on top of Connor in a very ungraceful way. I was clumsy even when I wasn't trying to be—and the sad part was, that seemed to be the only part of my Ro Com plan that was working out right.

"Who's in here?" the strange voice asked.

I hoped the low-lying fog would hide

us, but there was no way he hadn't seen us since we had been in spotlight. And I didn't want to spend too much time on the floor in my dress.

The lights dancing around us kept the doorway in shadow. I still couldn't see who was coming in, but I was pretty sure that whoever it was would know that we didn't have permission to be in the soundstage at ten o'clock on a Friday night.

"Who's out *there*?" Connor asked back as he helped me to my feet while I checked to make sure my dress had survived the fall.

"Maybe it's the cleaning crew," I whispered.

I hope. I hope. I hope.

"Security," the voice answered back.

No such luck.

Eleven

"Name?"

"Tracy Vance."

"And you work?"

"Part-time," I replied with my brightest please-don't-arrest-me smile.

"I mean, what department?"

"Oh," I said looking around the office. I have to admit, I was kind of nervous. I'd never been in a police station in my life. Not that this was like a regular police station.

The studio's security office was designed to look like a real police station on the outside so it could be used for filming. The entrance resembled one of those stations you'd find in an old gangster movie from the forties, with a stone facade and stairs leading up to the front door. But inside, it looked like any other office on the lot: a row of cubicles and fluorescent lighting. There wasn't even a cell.

But it still made me feel a bit like Paris Hilton. And not the party girl Paris, either. I mean the post-party, pre-penitentiary Paris.

I kept reminding myself that he was a security guard and not an actual police officer, so I wasn't under arrest. Still, the guard could call the cops, who *would* place me under arrest for trespassing.

The guards had been pretty cop-like in the way they separated Connor from me as soon as we got to the guard station. I'd last seen my date being led into a cubicle at the end of the hall.

"Well?"

"I'm sorry," I said, realizing he'd asked a question. "I'm a page."

He made a note on the form on his desk.

"I know we weren't supposed to be in the soundstage," I quickly added, "but the door was open and I guess we sort of got caught up in the moment."

"And decided to put together an impromptu light show?" the security guard asked in a way that indicated he wasn't even close to believing my story. "Wait here," he said before I could answer. He got up and went into the office at the end of the hall. I couldn't see what he was doing in there, but I doubted it was good for me.

I looked at the nameplate on the cubicle wall. His name was Perkins. I knew a lot of the security guards on the lot. It helped when trying to get permission for my tours to see some closed sets during the day. But this guy wasn't one of my friends. I'd never even seen him before—he probably just worked the night shift or something.

He kept me waiting in the cubicle for about five minutes. I guess he was trying to sweat the truth out of me by making me wait, or whatever it is they do on police dramas on TV. I don't know much about that. I'm more of a hospital show girl myself. Give me an obscure medical condition and mix it with some romantic tension and I'm good to go.

I realized my mind had been drifting again while Officer Perkins had been gone, so I brought myself back to the problem at hand. That kept me occupied for a moment, until I wondered whether or not it was appropriate to refer to a security guard as

"Officer." That line of thought kept me busy until he returned.

"The lights were already on, Officer Perkins," I lied before he could even ask a question. "That's what caught our attention. We didn't intend to be there, but we were curious."

"And this?" he asked, holding out the "Press Me" note.

"Maybe somebody left it there?" I suggested. Technically, that part was true. Somebody did leave it there. I wasn't about to tell him who that person was though. No reason to get Dex in trouble, even though, technically, it was his fault.

"Do you know how expensive that lighting equipment is?" Officer Perkins asked. "It's not a toy."

"Yes sir," I said, hoping the "sir" would earn me some points. The sneer that stayed on his face told me that it didn't.

A door slamming pulled us both out of the interrogation and made me even more anxious. Slamming doors were never a good sign. I wanted to pop up and see who was coming, but I didn't think Officer Perkins would have liked that.

I got my answer soon enough when my

boss, Carl, came huffing into the cube. He glanced at Officer Perkins and then glared at me. "Tracy," he said. "Care to tell me why I'm here?"

"They called you at home?" I asked in horror. If my boss had had to come back to work on a Friday night, there was no way I was walking out of there with my job. "Wait a minute. You live over the hill. How did you get here so fast?"

"You lucked out, Tracy," Carl said. "We've got that new game show taping tonight and I needed to be here in case the ushers have any problems with the audience."

I actually breathed a sigh of relief. I'd forgotten all about the game show. Thank the innovators of Hollywood for live studio audiences.

"Better question," Carl said. "What are *you* doing here?"

"Some kind of misunderstanding," I said with my best innocent act.

Officer Perkins still wasn't buying it. "Not a misunderstanding," he said. "Criminal trespassing."

I thought the *criminal* part was a bit overdramatic. At least, I hoped it was.

Carl looked way angrier than he had

been the night I disappeared with Christy Caldwell. If only she were with me in the cubicle to defend me to security. But I wasn't worried about myself at the moment.

"Wait a minute," I said to Officer Perkins. "You didn't call Connor's boss, did you?"

"She's gone for the night," he replied. I felt a huge weight lifted off my shoulders, until he added, "We haven't gotten a home number for her yet, but we're working on it."

This time, I did pop up out of my chair. I looked over the cube walls to the area where Connor was being interrogated. I couldn't see him, probably because he was in a chair. But I could see another guard's head, bobbing up and down in what I hoped was an understanding manner.

"Tracy?" Carl asked.

"You can't call his boss," I said. I couldn't let Connor get fired because of my plan. Well, to be precise, it was Dex's plan, but he had been doing me a huge favor, so it wasn't like I was going to blame him just because it didn't work out the way he'd intended. He wasn't in the lighting union yet, and they'd probably frown on him doing any unauthorized work at the studio.

"It was all me," I insisted. "I saw the open door and told Connor that I wanted to go inside. He said that we shouldn't, but I thought that was where the set for the new Spielberg movie was and I really wanted to see it. When we got in there, I realized it was the wrong soundstage. You know, it's so hard to tell them apart sometimes."

"But you're a tour guide," Officer Perkins said.

"It was dark," I said. "We don't give tours at night."

I looked at Carl to back me up, but he stood there, stone-faced. "Go on," he said with a nod.

"I saw this console," I said. "Just sort of sitting there. And the note. I don't know who the note was for, but I was curious. So I pressed the button."

"Do you go around randomly pushing buttons?" the guard asked.

"Sometimes she does," Carl added.

I couldn't tell if he was making a light joke or if he was being serious. I hoped for the best and pressed on with my story. "Then all this music started and the lighting went crazy. Connor told me we should leave, but I got all caught up in the moment and made him dance with me. He didn't want to, but I forced him."

"Held him there against his will?" Carl asked.

I glared at him. He was not making this any easier. But I swear I saw the slightest bit of a smile on his face.

"And you don't know who put together the light show?" Officer Perkins asked.

"Not a clue," I said. No reason to get Dex in trouble too.

"Okay," the guard said as he turned to Carl. "Let me see if these stories match and I can turn her over to you."

Carl nodded solemnly. All trace of a grin was gone, which only caused my nervousness to quadruple. I tried to send telepathic messages to Connor telling him my entirely false story, knowing the odds that he would pick up on my thoughts were astronomical, if not infinitely impossible.

Officer Perkins left me alone with my boss, which was almost worse than being with the guard. Carl's a great guy and I kind of consider him a friend, so I certainly didn't want to disappoint him. But I'd caused problems for him twice in one week, and that was not going to look very good in my employee file.

"So, that's your story," Carl asked, all serious and businesslike.

"Yes," I squeaked out in response.

"You do realize I could fire you over this?" he asked.

My eyes went wide.

"Or over the fact that you're still lying to me," he added.

"I'm not—"

"Please, Tracy," he said. "You're one of my best tour guides. You know exactly what movies are filming in what stages. You know what movies have filmed in what stages all the way back to the opening of Sovereign Studios. And you know that Steven Spielberg has never and probably will never film at this studio."

Okay, so maybe my lie wasn't entirely perfect.

"You're not the first page to ever sneak into a soundstage," Carl said. "And I'm pretty sure that you don't know enough about lighting systems to set up the show the guard told me about on the phone. So I can be fairly confident that you didn't mess with any expensive electrical equipment. Although . . . it is possible that you got someone to mess with it for you?"

"No sir," I said, hoping that he had partial amnesia and forgot that Liz's father was on the lighting staff and that her brother was an apprentice. "I just pressed a button."

Carl nodded like he wanted to believe me. "Probation," he said. "Two weeks working in the studio store."

"The Bric-a-brac Shack?" I blurted out without thinking. That was the worst assignment a page could get. I'd spend the entire day folding T-shirts and herding tourists to the bathroom while they waited for their tour guides to come and start the tour. It wasn't a hard job, just incredibly *boring*. But, still, I was getting off easy and I knew it.

So long as Connor told some kind of story that sounded remotely like mine.

"Or I could put you in the mailroom," Carl suggested.

The thought of two weeks with Mailroom Guy—the one who set me on this whole Operation Ro Com plan in the first place—was unbearable. "No," I said. "I'm happy to work in the studio store. Thank you for being so understanding."

"You two can get out of here," Officer Perkins interrupted as he walked Connor up to the cubicle we were in. "And don't make me say that I don't want to see either of you around here again."

I wasn't about to point out to him that he'd just said that very thing. I sprung up out of the chair and made for the exit. "Thanks!"

"Before we go," Carl said, placing a hand on my shoulder to keep me there. "I take it their stories matched?"

Officer Perkins gave a snort of a laugh. "This one refused to say anything," he sneered in Connor's direction. "Kept asking for his *lawyer*."

"Only following my dad's advice," Connor said, flashing a smile in my direction. "He told me that if I ever have a run-in with the law, I should not say anything until I have obtained proper representation."

I could see Carl holding back laughter. I took that as a very good sign.

"Get out of here," Officer Perkins said.

I thanked my boss one last time before blowing out of there with Connor. We didn't say a word for a full block, until Connor stopped us before we made the turn to the parking lot.

"You know, it's weird," he said. "In the time I've worked here, I've never been in the infirmary or in the security office before. And now I've been to both places in the past few days."

"I'm so sorry," I said. "I didn't think this would happen. I didn't think at all. It was a stupid plan. I'm so sorry we got in trouble."

Connor burst out laughing. "Are you kidding? That was *awesome*! The guard actually believed I knew a lawyer! I thought I was going to have to call one. How did you get us out of there?"

A wave of relief washed over me. Connor wasn't going to end our date on the spot. He didn't hate me for getting us in trouble. In fact, he'd enjoyed it!

"I just told the truth," I said. "Or a slightly altered version of the truth." I was proud of myself for getting us out of the jam. Not that I'd done much. But whatever I *had* managed to do had worked.

Although, a small part of me wondered why all Connor had come up with was insisting he be allowed to call his fictional lawyer. It wasn't exactly movie-star heroic of him. Not that I had expected him to break us out of the security office. But maybe insisting that he get some kind of punishment alongside my probation wouldn't have been horrible. . . . I never would have let him actually *get* punished, but the gesture would have been appreciated.

"This was like the most perfect date ever," Connor said. "And it's all because of you."

"You mean to say, I'm to blame."

"Yes," he said. "Yes, you are."

And then he leaned in to kiss me.

His kiss was a bit rougher than I'd expected, but once he realized I was kissing back, he relaxed into it more. We were finally having our moment. Maybe I'd put too much emphasis on it, but the kiss wasn't all I'd been hoping it would be. Kind of awkward, actually. It was only starting to get nice when I saw something out of the corner of my eye that distracted me, bringing the kiss to an abrupt end.

"Is something wrong?" Connor asked.

"No," I said, glancing past Connor to

confirm that I'd seen what I thought I'd seen. "It's just been a long night."

"I know," he said. "And it's not even eleven o'clock! Would you mind if we stopped by my building on the way to the car? I can get a better idea of how *Table for Two* is tracking on my computer."

"Why don't you go?" I said. "I want to stop by the office to check my probation schedule with Carl. I'll meet you at your car."

"Okay," he said as he hurried off. "See you there."

I waited until he was off in the distance. "You can come out now, bro," I called to Dex.

"Saw me, huh?" Dex said as he walked around the trailer he'd been hiding behind.

"Were you following us?"

"No . . . I mean, yes, but not the way you mean." Dex said. "I was hanging around outside the soundstage in case anything went wrong. Sorry I didn't see the security guard before he went inside."

"It's okay," I said.

"One of the light crew guys was working on that new show they're taping," Dex said. "He was heading on a break when he stopped to talk to me. When he left, I saw the guard taking you and Connor out of the stage. I followed you to the security office and was waiting to see what happened. If you were in there any longer I was going to go in and take the blame, but you came out with Connor and everything looked good."

I nodded.

"So . . . how was it?" he asked.

"Meh," I said. It was the best word I could come up with.

Dex looked deflated. "Really? I thought you would have liked it more."

"No! Not what you did," I quickly said. "The light show was amazing! It was more than amazing. It was like the most romantic thing I'd ever been a part of in my life."

The smile he had was beaming as bright as his light show.

"I meant that the date was 'meh'," I said.

"Oh," Dex said with a solemn nod. "So I guess the first-date curse continues?"

I thought about what he was asking me. "Meh" wasn't really all that bad. In fact, "meh" was better than I'd had in a long time. There was nothing inherently wrong with Connor. He didn't have a pirate fetish, horribly bad breath, or anything weird like that. And we didn't spend the entire evening talking about *him*, like some guys

I'd gone out with in the past. Being with Connor was kind of exciting, actually.

And I had the bruises and probation to prove it.

"No," I said, still considering my options. "I think there's definitely a second date in this. We're not at a relationship yet, but I'm not done trying."

Twelve

"Does lunch count as a second date?" I asked Liz while we stood in the hot food line at the commissary. It was Thursday, and Connor and I had lunched together the two other days I'd been trapped—I mean *scheduled*—working in the Bric-a-brac Shack and helping sell tours. I couldn't decide if I was in a relationship or if I still, technically, had not gotten past the first-date stage. I also couldn't decide between a burger and the fish entree.

"Depends on where you go, what you do, and who you're with," she said as the chef handed her a tasty looking stir-fry. "Personally, I don't think lunches at work, with your friends, squeezed in between guiding tourists to the restrooms is exactly date material."

"That's what I thought," I said as I pointed her dish out to the chef. "I'll have that."

Liz and I paid for the food and staked out a table in the dining area. The place was packed since some of the TV productions were starting up again. This was the third lunch I was scheduled to meet Connor for in the past week. One of us had run late for each lunch so far, so it was no surprise when Liz and I started eating before he got there.

Connor came in a few minutes later. It took some time before he saw me waving since Liz and I were nowhere near where we usually sat. Once he did see me, he practically ran to the table. His excitement was a nice surprise. Unfortunately, it had nothing to do with me.

"Guess what?" he said. "No, don't guess. You'll never guess. I'll tell you. The vice president of marketing couldn't decide on the ad campaign for that new thriller we still haven't settled on a title for."

I'd read the script for that movie. A title was the least of their concerns. In my mind, the plot was a much bigger issue.

"He called me into his office to show me

the two posters he had to choose between and asked me what I thought," Connor said. "And then he went with the one I picked!"

"That's great!" I said.

"Awesome," Liz agreed.

"But now he wants me in on the lunch meeting to talk about titles," Connor said, his mood deflating noticeably. "So I'm only here to pick up lunch and then head back to the office. Sorry."

"Oh, no problem," I said. "That's much more important."

"Maybe we can go out on Saturday to make up for it?"

And there it was. The official second date invite. My heart wasn't doing flip-flops or anything, but I was happy to get the pre-liminaries out of the way. Now, all I had to do was accept the date. That was the part where I typically ran into trouble. The heart said yes, but the mouth usually said no.

It's not like guys hadn't been interested in second dates before. It was the part where they hadn't been interest-*ing* that was the problem. And Connor was fairly interest-ing, himself. But not quite as interesting in the areas in which I was interested in having interest. If that makes any sense.

"Tracy?" Connor asked, checking his watch.

I looked up from my stir-fry. "Sorry," I said. "I drifted. Sure. Saturday it is."

"Considering how our first date ended, I'm totally leaving the plans up to you," he said. "Maybe we can get sent to a real police station this time."

"One can only hope," Liz said.

I pointed to the serving area. "The line's getting long." If he wanted to get back to the office quickly, he was going to have to get to the food before the next rush came in.

"Thanks," he said.

We both watched him walk off before Liz turned to me and said, "I'm sensing a certain lack of enthusiasm on your end."

"I guess."

"What's wrong? You got your relationship. Wouldn't you call that a success?"

I shrugged. "It is, but it doesn't feel the way I thought it would."

"Your heel doesn't pop when you kiss?" Liz asked, throwing in a *Princess Diaries* reference.

"Connor's a great guy and all," I replied, "but it's not quite . . ."

"Love?" Liz asked.

I nodded.

"You ever think the reason you never get past these first dates is that you don't give these guys enough of a chance?" Liz asked, gently. "These things do take time."

I nodded again. There was something to what she was saying. The problem with Operation Ro Com was that it was based on movie love parameters. And even the best romantic comedies barely lasted longer than two hours. So the question was, how did I adjust that to my—

"Time!" I shouted, dropping my fork into my stir fry and scaring the people at the table beside us.

"Um . . . what about it?" Liz asked.

"That's what I need!" I said, grabbing my notebook and flipping through the pages. What I was looking for was a couple of pages in, and it described exactly what my relationship required. "I have to move this relationship along. To get to that point where we're comfortable and not trying so hard."

"You're going to force yourselves to get comfortable?" Liz asked. "How do you plan that?"

"I need a montage."

"A montage?"

"A series of cute dating scenes cut together to show how much fun we're having in the relationship," I said. "Usually set to some ridiculously sentimental pop song destined to be a top forty hit."

"I know what a montage is," Liz said. "I've never heard of one in real life."

I couldn't explain any further because Connor was already back at the table. Turns out, he'd bypassed the line and gone straight for the prepackaged salads.

"Can we start our date Saturday morning?" I asked.

"Why?" he asked with an adorable smile. "What do you have in mind?"

"It's a surprise," I said. "But keep the entire day open."

"The *entire* day?" His smile widened.

Okay, how could I not give this relationship thing a try considering how eager he was?

"The entire day," I replied. I was sure I could come up with enough ideas to fill the day by Saturday. Especially if I had Liz and Dex help me.

Connor nodded his head, smiling broadly as he left the commissary.

Again, if my life were a movie, this would

be the point where the ridiculously senti-mental pop song would cue up and we'd cut to Saturday morning. . . .

We open on a shot of the blue-gray water of the Pacific Ocean.

My legs straddle a surfboard in the chilly water off the Malibu Coast. A hand-ful of surfers are in the water, but the beach is entirely empty. A light haze fills the air as the sun rises over the mountains along the shore.

Connor's hands hold the board steady while my legs fight off goose bumps. The ocean rises behind me. With Connor cheer-ing me on, I brace for my first attempt at standing on water. My mind races back over the lesson he'd given me on the shore.

Connor releases the board with an encouraging cheer as the water swells, about to break. At the moment the wave crashes, I push up off the board and hop into stand-ing position, trying the pose that Connor had shown me. I hold it for a fraction of a second until the board shoots out from under me.

I tumble backward into the water, feel-ing a sudden splash of reality. I dunk under and resurface. The leash of the board tugs against my ankle as I see Connor laughing.

Running my hand through the wet curls in my hair, I laugh with him.

Cut to . . .

Venice Beach.

The sun is up. The fog has burned off.

Connor and I rollerblade along the concrete path running along the sand. The path is full of tourists, families, and locals out for a morning stroll.

We blade past blankets spread out on the beach where artists sell their paintings, jewelry, and handcrafts. On the other side of the path, storefronts displaying tourist trinkets and designer knockoffs fly by. An old woman yells out to us, offering a reading from her psychic cat.

I reach out to grab Connor's hand. As our fingers touch, a shout draws our attention to the path ahead.

An out-of-control biker is heading in our direction, barreling down at an out-of-control speed. Connor and I break apart in time for the biker to pass, then reconnect, laughing all the way.

With our hands firmly locked, we fall

into step, developing a rhythm that was sorely lacking when we tried dancing a week earlier. We glide along the pathway passing joggers and cyclists—and other couples like ourselves, holding hands and rolling along.

Cut to . . .

My hand bangs into Connor's as we both reach into the bag of popcorn at the same time.

I turn to face him in the dim light from the movie screen and we share a smile. Connor waves his hand over the bag to let me go first. I take a few pieces of popcorn and settle into my seat, munching quietly.

Onscreen, *Table for Two* plays. Christy Caldwell is running around the kitchen of a restaurant making meals for a dozen people all by herself. Connor's already seen it a bunch of times, but he laughs along with me as if it's the first time he's seen her slip on the rolling pin. Her male costar comes in and catches her as a shower of freshly peeled shrimp rain down on them from the bowl she'd been carrying.

I reach over for a handful of popcorn and brush against Connor's hand again.

We share another smile as Connor hands the bag over to me.

Cut to . . .

A gray metal cart rolls through a Chinese restaurant.

We're sitting at a table for two in the middle of a huge, crowded room. Waitresses push various carts with dim sum delicacies for the patrons to choose from. Appetizer-size plates fill the tables at the packed restaurant.

Connor stops the waitress to get a look at the food on her cart before making his selection. At first, I can't see what he's choosing, but I turn away once the plate is placed on the table. Chicken feet look about as appetizing as the name implies.

I can feel Connor holding the plate out to me. My face scrunches up tighter than the curls in my hair as I shake my head. Connor playfully reaches around and dangles a chicken's foot in front of my eyes. He grabs a second one and makes them dance around the table, causing me to burst out in laughter.

An elderly Asian couple at the next table watches us, whispering to each other with grins on their faces. I imagine they have been together for decades and wonder if that is where Connor and I are heading.

Cut to . . .

The sun is setting over the mountains.

We ride on horseback along the trails at Griffith Park. I can't see the observatory from where we're riding, but I know it's there, sitting on the edge of a hill as a silent reminder of the first date to end all first dates.

I push my parents out of my mind.

Connor and I ride side by side out of the area recently burned by fires and into the lush and green section that remained untouched by the flames. A pair of chipmunks playfully scamper along the path ahead of us. They run off together into the brush, leaving us alone on the path with our horses. Among the trees, with no one around, it's like we're in a forest miles from civilization, rather than a couple of hundred yards from the freeway.

Connor reaches out and grabs an orange flower off the branch of a nearby tree. It goes perfectly with my blouse. He hands me the flower. It smells like the first perfume my mom ever let me wear. Somehow I manage to twist the flower into what remains of the curls in my hair.

Cut to . . .

Home.

Connor walks me to my front door, carrying the bag with my beach clothes for me. I briefly consider inviting him inside until I see both my parents' cars in the driveway. Connor doesn't seem to mind, though. He doesn't even question it when I stop at the steps and turn to him, making it clear that the date has come to an end.

"This was an amazing day," he says, touching the flower still in my hair.

"Amazing," I agree, for lack of a better word.

"You are, by far, the most fun girl I've ever gone out with," he says. "Seriously."

"Thanks," I say.

"See you on Monday?"

"I'm not on the schedule until Tuesday," I say. "But I'll call you."

"Yeah," Connor says, leaning forward.

I move in and we share our second kiss. It isn't as rough as the first, but it still doesn't feel quite right to me. There must be something off with our timing, or the angle of our heads, or something.

I doubt he notices it. The look on his face as we break apart seems to suggest that he enjoyed himself.

"See you Monday," he says as he hands me my bag.

"Tuesday," I correct him.

"Yeah, Tuesday."

"Bye," I say.

The music in the montage of my mind swells. I sigh and lean against the front door as I watch him pull away.

Fade to black.

Thirteen

"Montages are exhausting," I said to myself as I closed the door behind me and turned off the outside light.

"Is that you, dear?" Dad called from the living room, immediately causing my spidey senses to tingle. Something was up. I could tell in the oh-so-innocent tone of his voice, and his use of the word "dear."

I walked into the living room to find my parents lying on opposite ends of the couch. Mom's feet were draped across Dad's lap while he was massaging them. She was holding a book and he was watching TV with the sound on low. They both had matching smiles and were going out of their way to look like they weren't up to something, which told me that they were.

"Did you have a nice date?" Mom asked.

"Fine," I said, cautiously.

"I trust that the young man was well-behaved," Dad said, like we were in some old fifties sitcom.

"Yes," I said, still trying to figure out what was going on.

"And did he walk you to the door like a proper gentleman?" Mom asked.

At this point, I realized the book she was reading was upside down. "You were watching!"

"We don't know what you're talking about," Dad said.

I stomped across the room, ripped the book out of Mom's hand, and showed them that I saw it was upside down. She wasn't that dumb. She did that on purpose. "You wanted me know!"

My parents burst out laughing and gave each other high fives before settling back into their relaxed poses.

"Why do you torment me?" I asked. Being an only child, my parents liked to remind me what it would be like to have a sibling every now and then by messing with me in a way that only an older sister or a younger brother would.

"Your boyfriend can walk you all the way up to the front door and he can't even come in for a moment to meet the parents?" Mom asked, with a hint of seriousness under her joking tone.

"He's not my boyfriend," I said. "We just started going out."

"Still," Mom continued. "You rush out of here first thing in the morning, then you won't even let him say hi to us when he brings you home? Why, in our day—"

"You don't have to tell me about 'your day.' I've read all about it," I said, pointing to the frame on the wall that had a photo of them on their first date along with the cover page of Uncle Earl's *True Love* script.

"Trace," Dad said. "We were just playing around. There's no need—"

"I'm sorry," I said, not quite sure why I'd exploded at them like that. "It's been a long day. I'm going to bed." Even though it was only nine o'clock, I headed down the hall to my room, dropped my bag on the bed, and picked up the phone, dialing Liz.

"Hey," she said as a gigantic explosion

went off behind her and the sound of gun-fire rattled over the phone line.

"Whoa. Did I interrupt a war or some-thing?"

"I'm in the middle of whupping Dex's butt on Halo," she said, before adding a "Die, scum!"

I heard Dex yell "Hi, Trace!" through the phone.

I took the phone away from my ear and stared at it for a moment, wondering how I could be best friends with someone so very different from myself. "You want to call me back?"

"Nah," she said. "I can do both. How was your montage?"

"Exhausting," I said. "I don't know what writers are thinking when they put them in movies."

"You're not supposed to do a montage all in one day," Liz said. "In movies they. repre-sent time passing. A relationship growing. Forcing them into one Saturday . . . well, it's just ridicu— Hey!"

"Ha!" I heard Dex yelled. "Eat lead!"

"How else am I supposed to know if Connor's the guy for me?" I asked, ignoring the battle in the background. I opened up my bag, took my beach clothes out, and dumped them in my hamper.

"I think the fact that he's put up with you this long is a good sign."

"Put up with me? He's loved every minute of it."

"What wouldn't he love?" she asked. "You're doing all this fun stuff. *I'd* love it if a guy I was with wanted to do all these things you're doing. Most guys I've dated just want to sit at home and watch TV."

"Then why don't I love it?" I asked.

"Maybe Connor's not the guy for you," Liz said.

"But he's perfect on paper," I insisted as I changed into pajamas. "Just run down the stats. Willing to hang with me and my friends—well, that would be mainly you. Happy to do whatever I want, but secure enough to suggest his own things. Loves his job, so he's mostly positive and not all gripey and complaining. My parents are dying to meet him, but I'm not ready for that yet."

Silence.

"Liz?"

"Sorry. Dex just ambushed me. Hold on one second."

I put down the phone as I changed my

top. When I picked up the phone again, I could hear the rat-a-tat of gunfire and explosions coming over the line before a silence that was followed by Dex going, "Awwww." I took that to mean the game was over.

Liz picked up the phone and continued our conversation.

"Okay," she said. "Tell me about this montage date from the beginning."

I rewound the day and shared every minute of my montage with her. When I mentioned *Table for Two*, we got sidetracked for a few minutes while we dissected the film. (She hated the scene where Christy's character was dressed in a slutty waitress uniform. I was more bothered by the script's blatant similarities to *Room for Rent*. We both loved the new ending because it was ridiculously romantic when Christy's male costar found her the perfect spot to open her own restaurant.)

Once we got back on track, we spent the better part of an hour going over every tiny detail of my newfound relationship. By the end of the hour, I had come to the conclusion that I knew my friend was too kind to point out.

Something was wrong with me.

There had to be. There was nothing I wanted more than a relationship with a great guy. I had the great guy. I had the relationship. I had everything I wanted, but I still wasn't enjoying it.

This is the problem with real life. When a girl is with the wrong guy in movies, there are clear signs that he's not right for her. He's obviously cheating on her with some skank. Or he's so busy that he blatantly ignores her all the time, leaving her waiting for him out in the rain. Or he kicks cute little puppies.

But Connor didn't do any of those things. At least, I was pretty sure he didn't. It was weird that I was almost wishing I could see him around small animals just to give me a real reason things couldn't work out between us.

"He is great, isn't he?" I asked without realizing I was talking out loud.

"Way great," Liz agreed.

"I need to learn to appreciate him more."

"Yes. You do."

"I need him to break up with me."

The phone went dead for a moment. "What?"

"The breakup is basic to the plot of any romantic comedy. Girl meets boy. Girl *loses* boy. Girl gets boy back. Think of Drew Barrymore in *Music and Lyrics*, think of Drew in *Never Been Kissed*, think of her in *Ever After*."

"Maybe it's not Ro Coms, maybe it's just Drew."

I ignored her. "I need to break up with Connor so I can learn to appreciate him."

"And how do you plan to do that?" she asked. I could hear the reluctance in her voice.

"Oh, I've got an idea."

Again, if this were a movie, the camera would now tighten in on my mischievous grin.

Fourteen

I wished my hair wasn't so short. It wasn't the first time I'd had that wish since the flat-iron fiasco, but at least now the reasoning was different. Whenever I was stressed, I used to play with my hair to calm me. I'd absentmindedly stretch out my tight curls and it would have this calming effect as I pulled my hair down past my shoulders and felt it bounce back into place. I hadn't realized how much I missed that nervous habit until this moment.

"This is stupid," I said. "I can't believe how stupid this is."

"Well, it was your idea," the ever-helpful Liz said. Not that she was wrong or anything. It was totally my idea, but I was going to need both of my closest friends to help pull it off. This was going to be the hardest phase of Operation Ro Com.

"It's not too late to call it off," Liz added from the couch. She'd only agreed to take part in this plan if I promised to make it the absolute last thing I ever did as part of my plan to find love. I didn't blame her. It was going to be a little cruel to Connor. But, if it finally made me appreciate him and learn to love him, then it would all be worth it in the end.

Dex was also reluctant to help. But once I explained to him how he could look at the situation as an acting exercise, he got more into it. I even promised that, if he did me this favor, I'd help him rehearse his lines for his play whenever he asked. (Honestly, I would have done that anyway, but it was a useful negotiating tool.)

"I should call it off," I said as I paced in the page break room, the setting for my ingeniously ridiculous plot. The place was abandoned except for the three of us. Everyone else was at lunch. I was pretty sure we had the place to ourselves for at least an hour since no one ever took a break from lunch. And my plan wouldn't take even half that time. "Do you think I should call it off?"

Liz opened her mouth to respond, but I didn't give her the chance.

"Never mind," I said. "I know what you think. I have to do this. It's the only way. I spent the last day and a half thinking about this. It needs to be done. And I'm going to do it."

"Do you need the two of us here for this?" Liz asked.

"Don't you go anywhere," I insisted. Then I realized that if my plan was going to work, she had to leave. "Okay, well, you can go. But go where I need you to go. And then come right back." As an afterthought, I added, "Please."

Liz got up from the couch with an exaggerated sigh. "Should we synchronize our watches?"

"You're taking great pleasure from my pain," I said.

"Yes," she agreed. "Yes, I am."

"Go," I said, pointing to the door.

Once Liz was gone, I resumed my pacing. It was a contained pace since the page break room was only about ten feet by ten feet. The joke was that we pages never got much of a break from anything. Ha. Ha.

Dex got up from the couch and stood in front of me. With a row of lockers on my right and the couch on my left, he pretty much cut off my pacing route. "We can still call this off if you want to," he said.

"Why?" I said in a panic. "Don't you want to do it?"

"No," he quickly replied. "I'm happy to help you. I just thought that you—"

"I know. I'm sorry," I said. "I'm freaking out."

"Yes. That you are."

"Pace with me," I said.

"I'll try." Dex threw an arm around me as we made the ten-foot walk back and forth across the room. The turns were a little tight, but it felt good. He always has a calming effect on me.

"Thanks for helping me with this," I said.

"No, you were right," he replied. "It will be a good acting exercise."

"You know I just made that excuse up, right?"

"Either way, I'm here for you," he said. "Now. Feel better?"

"Much," I said, checking my watch. Liz had been gone long enough to get to the commissary and find Connor. "We should get in position."

"Oh," Dex said. "Okay."

We stepped toward each other, but stopped. I guess neither one knew how to make the next move. Funny that he'd just had his arm around me, in friendship, but now we were being all awkward.

I started us off by putting my hand on his shoulder. His wince suggested that maybe I'd slammed my palm down a little too hard. I gently slid it down his arm. I could feel him shaking. "You okay?" I asked.

"Yeah, it's . . . this is weird."

"I know."

Dex leaned in, then abruptly pulled back like he'd gone too far into my personal space or something. If this was going to work, that was exactly what he was going to have to do, so I pulled him toward me. I guess I was stronger than I thought, because he slammed into me and we actually bounced off each other.

That broke us both into hysterics.

"This is silly," I said, pulling Dex into me, more gently this time.

Our bodies relaxed as our arms wrapped around each other. It felt just like it did when we danced together at the prom. If everything went according to plan, Connor would walk in on me and Dex in what looked to be a tight embrace. Actually, it *was* kind of a tight embrace.

"Better?" I asked.

Dex sighed. "Much."

We kind of stood there for a moment with nothing to say. The silence was weird, but it didn't feel wrong. Still, I thought I should say something. "So, how are things with you and the actress?"

"Didn't work out," he said. "She was mad that I got a part in the play and she didn't."

"Oh," I said.

More silence.

"Liz should be bringing Connor here any moment," I said with a glance toward the door.

"And you think this is going to help your relationship?" Dex asked. "Him seeing you in my arms?"

"I think it's going to help *me*," I said.

"You are an odd person."

I stiffened. Liz said that to me all the

time, but there was something different about the way it sounded coming from Dex. "You think so?"

"I didn't mean it as an insult," Dex said. "Odd is good. I like odd. But I don't get why you think how anything good can come out of Connor walking in on you and me together."

"I need to learn to appreciate what I've got," I said. "All these guys I've gone out with . . . the relationships never go anywhere. I used to think it was the guys. We've all had a lot of fun blaming the guys and coming up with nicknames for them. But maybe it's me. Maybe I don't know how to love anyone. If I lose Connor, I might finally figure out what I'm missing."

"If you love something, set it free," Dex said with a nod. "Is that what you're thinking?"

"Something like that," I said. It was nice to have someone who finally got me. Just because Liz was helping out didn't mean she was actually going along with me. "Clichés exist for a reason," I said.

"Maybe you haven't found the right guy yet," Dex suggested, gently rubbing my arm.

"That's my point exactly," I said. "Connor *is* the right guy. He's got to be the right guy."

"Where did all this desperation come from? This is not like you. You've had boyfriends before. You've been single before. Why are you so crazy about a relationship all of the sudden? It is because of your parents?"

I shook my head in shock. "What? Why would you say that? Just because I haven't introduced them to Connor yet—"

"I didn't know that," Dex said, grabbing on to me. I hadn't realized that I'd been pulling away from him. "I was talking about how you are trying so hard to make this into some big romance instead of just letting it happen. Your parents have this epic romance. Half of Hollywood has read about it, even. That's got to be a lot of pressure for you."

I thought about what he was saying. It made sense. Leave it to Dex to know me better than I knew myself. I looked into his eyes as we stood inches apart and finally felt comfortable with myself for the first time in a while. There was no rush to find the perfect guy. I still had my whole life in front of me.

"When did you get all smart and insightful?" I asked.

He shrugged, raising my arms along with his. "My parents have been happily dysfunctional longer than yours have. I kind of understand the pressure it puts on a kid."

"Thanks," I said as I gave him a big hug, which was pretty easy since we were already locked in an embrace.

"Um . . . you're welcome," he said as he flushed red.

Then I remembered what we were doing. I lifted my arm off his shoulder and checked my watch. "Shouldn't they be here by now?"

He turned us to the door. "You want me to check?"

"No," I said, holding him tight. "They might come in the moment you let go. We've got to stay in our pose so they can walk in on us."

"Why?"

"What?"

"Didn't we just agree that you don't need to find the perfect guy?" Dex asked. "So why do you still need to do this?"

"You make a good point," I replied, still holding onto him. I had never been this close to Dex for this long before. Even when we were dancing at the prom, it was usually one slow dance and then back to hanging with Liz. This hug had been stretching on a while. Can't say that I entirely minded. I'd never noticed the little flecks of gold in his green eyes before. They reminded me of the dancing lights from the romantic date he had set up for me.

And his face was only inches from mine. . . . Closer, really, than he'd even been to me before. It was all I could focus on.

I hardly even heard the door open behind us as our mouths pressed together.

"Tracy?!"

Connor's voice jolted me out of the kiss. I pulled back, shocked to see him beside us even though I had expected him all along. The look of surprise was mirrored by everyone in the room.

My stomach fell as I realized exactly how cruel my plan had been. It had seemed harmless when it was simply part of Operation Ro Com. But whatever it was I had shared in that moment with Dex made me realize how wrong that whole thing had been.

The look of hurt and pain on Connor's face made me physically ill.

"Connor!" I said.

My boyfriend turned away from me, pushing his way past Liz as he ran out the door.

"I'm sorry," I said to Dex as I stepped away from him.

"Tracy?" Liz said as I moved toward her.

"I'm sorry," I said. "You were right. This was dumb. I shouldn't have—"

The screech of tires stopped me mid-sentence. I can only imagine that the look of horror in Liz's eyes mirrored my own.

The three of us rushed out of the break room, across the hall, and out the front of the building.

An electric cart with a terrified driver behind the wheel was stopped in the middle of the roadway. Connor was lying in front of the cart, holding his left arm and writhing in pain.

This was *not* the way my plan was supposed to end.

Fifteen

I hate hospitals.

I hate them even more than I hate motion picture–studio infirmaries.

Even more than I hate motion picture–studio security offices.

But not nearly as much as I hated myself in that moment.

"Maybe he's got amnesia," I said as I paced the ER waiting room. "That's kind of a romantic comedy device, isn't it? The guy gets amnesia and the girl has to nurse him back to health. Then he falls in love with her all over again so that when he remembers how she broke his heart it doesn't matter anymore. That could happen in real life, right?"

"It could," Liz said. "But it didn't. I talked to him in the ambulance. He remembers everything."

I cringed at the mention of the ambulance. This time Connor's injury was more serious than a simple trip to the infirmary. I'd wanted to go along with him, but knew that it would just be a reminder of what he'd walked in on: Me and Dex locked in a . . . well, I wasn't entirely sure what we were locked in. But I really wasn't worrying about that at the moment.

I'd sent Liz in my place in the ambulance since someone needed to go with him. The EMTs had said that it didn't look serious, but any time flashing lights and a siren are involved, you know it's going to be more than a Big Bird Band-Aid and a lollipop.

Thankfully, Dex had offered to drive me to the hospital. I wasn't sure that behind the wheel of a car was the best place for me in the state I was in. I'd almost killed my sort-of ex-boyfriend, before he'd even had the chance to break up with me. Suddenly, I had become the same kind of Psycho Loser ex-girlfriend we always made fun of.

Dex was even kind enough to wait in the car instead of coming inside. There was only so much insult I was about to add to Connor's injury.

"He's never going to forgive me," I said.

"You wanted him to break up with you," Liz reminded me in the most sunshiny, chipper mood that she could fake. She was flipping through a waiting-room magazine that I knew she was only pretending to read. I could tell that she wanted to say something more, but was holding back.

"Yes, break up with me," I said. "Not break his arm in the process. I feel responsible."

"Could be because you are," she said with another flip of the page.

"Harsh!"

"True!"

"Okay," I said. "You're right. I'll just go in there, apologize, and we can go our separate ways."

"Finally!" Liz said, dropping the magazine on the table beside her.

I turned to the doors leading to the examination area. Other loved ones were going in and out, so I guessed it would be okay for me to go in too. Not that I considered myself a "loved one." I watched the doors while Liz stood with me in silence as the various patients in the ER moaned or chatted around us.

"You're not going anywhere," Liz pointed out.

I remained there, facing the double doors. "Maybe he doesn't want to see me."

"He does," Liz said, giving me a little shove in the direction of the examination room. "I can't imagine why."

I walked through the waiting room toward the treatment area. No one was stopping me, so I took that as a good sign. Once I passed through the doors, I could see Connor at the far end, leaning back on the bed with his eyes closed. His arm was already in a cast, resting across his stomach.

I took the long walk toward Connor, keeping my eyes straight ahead and focused. If I let him out of my sight for a moment, I was afraid I would turn and run away. I was just glad that his eyes were closed, so he wasn't watching me the whole time. I didn't think I could look him in the eyes yet, but I knew I had to be ready because I was pretty much out of options.

Connor looked so peaceful in the hospital bed, especially since he wasn't yelling at me.

Not that he'd ever yelled at me during our brief relationship, but I'd never given him a reason to before. Now I'd given him a couple of reasons, all in the span of a minute.

I was standing over him for a good thirty seconds before his eyes flitted open. "I thought I felt someone hovering," he said.

I got right to the point. "I'm sorry," I said. "What you walked in on . . . it wasn't . . . it didn't . . . you shouldn't have seen that." Too late, I realized that I should have asked him how he was feeling before hitting him with the apology.

"I feel like such an idiot," Connor said.

I guess that answered my question in a way. "Don't," I said. "It's not your fault."

"Of course it is," he replied, raising his cast. "I shouldn't have run out of there like that. It was stupid. And . . . come on . . . even a five-year-old knows you have to look both ways before you cross the street. Dumb." He smacked himself on the forehead with his cast. "Ow!"

I stifled my laugh. "But me and Dex—"

"Yeah, that was tough," Connor said. "I thought you and him were just friends."

"We are," I said a little too forcefully. "I

mean . . . that was . . . that's never happened before. You have to believe me."

"Okay."

That was a bit easier than I'd expected. "You believe me?"

"Are you lying to me?"

"No."

"Okay."

"Really?"

Connor had that cute confused look on his face. "We've had two dates. They were great dates. Amazing dates. But hardly a commitment. If you were seeing Dex also, I wish you would have told me. I would have told you if I was seeing anyone. But I'm not going to be mad about it."

"I'm not seeing Dex," I said. "That was a one-time thing. An accident."

He nodded.

Wow. He really was the *perfect* guy. But I kind of understood what he was saying. He didn't know I was trying to make this into a serious relationship. He was just going on a couple of dates, waiting to see where it would lead. We hadn't said we loved each other. He hadn't even met my parents yet.

"Do you want an exclusive commitment?" I asked without thinking. It isn't every day that you find someone that understanding. And that cute. He really was the total package.

The smile on Connor's face gave me my answer. "Do *you*?"

I looked down at him all broken in the hospital bed. The simple answer was yes. I did want to be in a relationship; an exclusive, committed, relationship. I still wasn't sure that I wanted that relationship to be with Connor, but what were the odds I'd find another guy as decent as him?

Whatever that thing with Dex was . . . he was my bro. (Okay, Tracy, mental note: stop with the "bro." It really does sound lame.) I'd never really thought of him as anything more than that before. He'd always been with Psycho Loser or getting over her. Whatever happened earlier could have just been a weird out-of-body experience-type thing where Dex was getting too deep into the part he was playing. I didn't want to risk losing whatever I could have with Connor over a case of Dex being a method actor.

Unable to give voice to all the thoughts swirling around my brain, I finally said, "Maybe. But why would you want to date me?"

That question didn't sound half as insecure and pathetic in my head.

"Are you kidding?" he asked. "Breaking into soundstages. Surfing. Horseback riding. Hospitals. Security guards." He was using the fingers on his good hand to count off our illustrious dating history. "This is some of the most fun I've had with anyone. My only regret is I'm still one scar behind Liz, but if you and me stay together I'm pretty sure I can overtake her."

"Well, that's something," I said, laughing.

"Pull up a chair and sit with me until they get around to signing me out," Connor said. "I've got a friend coming to pick me up. You can get a ride with us, unless you drove."

"No, that's okay," I said. "I got a ride. . . . Liz can go back that way. I'll go tell her."

"Don't be long," Connor said.

"Wouldn't think of it." Not that thinking was something I'd been doing all that much lately. I turned and went out to the waiting room.

I couldn't believe I'd gone in there ready to be dumped. The whole plan, in fact, had been constructed with that one goal in mind.

Yet, there I was, still in a relationship with an amazingly awesome guy who I wasn't sure I loved.

But that didn't mean I couldn't grow to love him.

I guess that the shock must have registered on my face because Liz looked concerned when she saw me coming back into the waiting room.

"That bad?" she asked.

"He let me off the hook."

"He let you off the hook?" she said way louder than necessary for a public emergency room. Several of the sick and wounded looked in our direction. I gave them all a smile before turning my attention back to Liz.

"He wants a relationship," I said.

"Yeah," she said. "You were the one up in the air on that. Which is why you were going to have him dump you."

"How could I?" I asked, glancing back to the treatment area. "I broke him. I should at least stay with him until he's healed. Maybe by then I'll come to love him. That was the point of this . . . kind of."

"And what about Dex?" she asked, seeming angrier than I would have expected.

"He's in the car."

"No!" Liz said again. "I walked in on that almost-kiss, too."

"That was all staged," I whispered. "You know that. You were in on it."

"It didn't look staged to me."

"We're just friends," I insisted. "Come on, I've known Dex as long as I've known you. He's like my brother."

"Yeah, well, he *is* my brother," Liz said. "And he never held me like that."

"Okay, eww," I said. "Don't need that mental picture."

"You're impossible," she said.

"That I am," I agreed. "Look, I'm going to catch a ride home with Connor and his friend. Could you . . ." I wasn't sure how to finish that sentence. I didn't know what I wanted her to say to Dex.

"I'll tell him you're going home with Connor," Liz said with a huff.

"Thank you," I said. I'd already caused enough hurt for one day. Not that I was sure Dex was hurting. He was probably as weirded out by what happened as I was.

I gave Liz a hug, but I didn't feel much of a squeeze in return from her. I imagine it can be kind of draining to be my friend at times. Then again, the grief I put her through is nothing compared to her expecting me to watch her jump out of a plane on her birthday. Talk about insane plans.

Once Liz was gone, I went back to sit with my boyfriend.

Sixteen

"I got it!" I screamed as I flew out of my bedroom and nearly knocked my dad over running for the front door. I was just glad that my house was all on one floor. If I had to run down the stairs like at Liz's house, I never would have beaten my parents to the foyer.

I paused and took a breath before opening the door. I could see Connor's shadow through the clouded glass. The cast on his arm was the only thing that kept it from being the perfect silhouette.

When I opened the door, I saw that he was holding a small bouquet of pink lilies in his good hand.

"Hi," I said, giving him a kiss along with my greeting.

"Hello," he said after the kiss ended. I guess he caught me staring at the flowers, because he quickly added. "For your mom. I thought it would make for a good ice-breaker. She's not allergic, is she?"

I shook my head. Little did he know. I looked at the flowers and the wrapping around the stems with the familiar starburst design. "Piccolo's," I said. "Good choice. They always have the freshest selection."

He had that adorable perplexed look on his face again, but didn't question me on how I guessed where he'd made his purchase. "So . . . are you going to let me in?"

"No," I said. "I figured we could hang out here all night." Part of me liked that plan a lot.

"That's no way to treat a guest," My mom said as she came up behind me. "Connor, get in here."

"Yes, ma'am," he said.

"Here's a tip," Mom said. "Calling a woman—particularly *this* woman—ma'am is not a good way to make a first impression. Makes me feel old. My name is Jennifer."

"Sorry, Jennifer," Connor said as he came into my home. "That's just how I was raised."

"Well, then I guess I can't fault you for it," Mom said as she took him by the arm and led him to the living room. "Connor, this is my husband. You may call him Tom, or you may call him sir, since he *is* old."

"I'm only a few months older than you, *dear*," Dad said as he reached out to shake Connor's hand. Considering one hand was holding flowers and the other was in a cast, they weren't very successful at this. "Those for me?" Dad asked.

"No, sir, um . . . I mean, Tom. They're for Jennifer." Connor deftly passed the flowers off to Mom and then swiveled back and shook Dad's hand. Mom looked at me and winked, giving me her silent approval of his smooth moves.

"Hm," she said as she went into the dining room to get one of her many vases out of the china cabinet. "Piccolo's. Nice call."

Dad directed Connor to the couch and I joined him there while we made small talk. I couldn't figure out why I was so nervous. Connor was the first guy I'd brought around to meet my parents in a while, but he wasn't the first guy *ever*. And it wasn't like I was expecting any similarities to the movie *Meet the Parents* since my parents were way more laid back than their fictional counterparts. No lie-detector tests in my house.

I mostly sat and listened while Dad and Connor talked about their jobs. Since I knew what they both did for a living—and they certainly knew what I did—I felt like I didn't have much to contribute to the conversation.

Mom returned with the crystal vase I'd given my parents on their twentieth anniversary a few months back. Everyone commented how the flowers looked beautiful in the tall vase when she placed it on the side table. Unfortunately, that also drew Connor's eyes to the wall . . . and the picture.

My head naturally fell into my hands when he got up for a closer look at the photo in the frame beside the cover page of Uncle Earl's magnum opus, *True Love.* "I read this," Connor said. "It's, like, the most romantic screenplay ever."

"Thank you," my parents said.

Again with the perplexed look. My parents shared a smile and broke into their tale. After a couple of decades, they were pretty good at co-storytelling, filling each other's pauses and finishing one another's sentences. I sat back and listened, like I always did.

I felt like a scientist observing animals in the wild as I watched the conversation without contributing much. The topic wound from the unsold screenplay, to movies in general, and back to Connor's marketing work.

Connor handled himself spectacularly well, which was no surprise. He loves to talk about his job, so he never ran out of subject matter, but he also asked all the right questions and listened politely while my parents spoke. He even laughed at Dad's lame jokes in a totally believable—and not at all forced—way. The doorbell, thankfully, interrupted Dad when he was in the middle of his Arnold Schwarzenegger impression, which is always embarrassing and not half as good as he thinks it is.

"Dinner's here," Mom said as she rose from the couch. She grabbed her purse and went for the door. Connor even stood up politely like the gentleman that he is, which actually made Dad look a little rude for not treating his own wife with the same respect. Naturally, Dad simply laughed it off rather than be embarrassed by it and remained firmly in his seat.

When Mom came back through the living room with the food, she asked me to help her set the table for dinner. I looked to Connor, but Dad assured me that they'd be all right. Since they seemed to be handling things well enough on their own, I joined Mom in the kitchen.

"What's on the menu?" I asked as I detected a hint of spice from the containers mom had unloaded onto the counter.

"Thai," Mom said as she pulled plates out of the cabinet. "Aren't you going to ask me what I think of Connor?"

No one can ambush you with a question like my mom.

"I can pretty much tell from the way you guys have been treating him," I whispered back. Not that my parents would have been rude to a guy they didn't like, but Dad would never have broken out the Schwarzenegger. He thinks that should be reserved for special guests.

I think it should be reserved forever.

"Well, just to make it formal," Mom said, laying a hand on my shoulder. "Your father and I approve."

No shock there.

"Mom, can I ask you a question without you reading too much into it and making a big deal?"

"I make no promises," she replied as she started spooning our meal out onto the plates.

"You and Dad," I said. "How did you know he was the one? I've read Uncle Earl's script a dozen times, and I can never tell when it happened. Was it the first date at the observatory? When you took him on the midnight sail to Catalina? The way he proposed on the Santa Monica Pier with the flying formation of doves overhead?"

Mom laughed. "The doves didn't really happen," she explained. "Your father didn't actually train birds to fly in a heart formation. That would be impossible. They were a bit of artistic license on Earl's part."

"Good to know," I said as I snatched a shrimp from my plate. "I always thought Dad had too much time on his hands. But seriously, at what point did you know he was the one?"

She held the serving spoon in the air as she thought about my question. "You're assuming there was one thing," Mom said. "Or that it was a thing at all."

Now *I* was working the perplexed look. "But the script—"

"Tracy, why do you think that after two decades Earl is an English teacher and that script hasn't sold?"

"Because no one believes two people as sappy as you and Dad can exist in the real world."

"Sort of," Mom said. "That script is about the things your Dad and I did for each other when we were first together. It's not really about how we fell in love. That's a more personal story. One that we would never let anyone share in a film script."

"Okay, then. How about sharing it with your daughter?"

Mom seemed to consider my question before she put down the spoon and picked up a couple of plates. "I could tell you," she said. "And I'm sure I will someday. But I think you're asking me because you want to know what to look for in your relationship. And sorry, but you're on your own there."

Mom left me alone in the kitchen with the remaining two plates. I couldn't believe she was just going to leave me hanging like that. She was right, of course. I had to figure out what I was looking for in a guy for myself. But still, a hint would have been helpful. We do share the same genes, after all.

I followed with the other plates, thinking over what she had said. There was still time for me to fall in love with Connor. He wasn't in any rush. If anything, he was being totally patient with me. Who's to say I couldn't grow to love him like my mom grew to love my dad?

Of course, it would probably be easier if Dex didn't keep popping into my mind.

Seventeen

Things between Connor and me continued along for the next week with very little change in the relationship, which in itself was a significant change. I finally accepted that I *was* in a relationship. We'd had several dates. Talked on the phone every night before bed. Met at the coffee cart on the paseo on the mornings I worked. It was just what I'd wanted from Operation Ro Com . . . except not.

It was like I was still waiting for that moment to happen. The one thing that would prove I was in love; the pop of a heel, or the fireworks when we kissed. I was giving it more time with this guy than I'd ever given anyone before, and still *nothing*.

Of course, questions about Dex and that kiss that I still didn't know what to make of kept lingering in my mind. It had been far too brief for me to have any kind of reaction other than confusion. And I couldn't even talk to Dex about it because I'd hardly seen him in the past week. I guess his schedule had changed because he rarely seemed to be around, which did give me time to concentrate solely on Connor.

Not that that was a good thing.

Because when my focus was totally on Connor all I could think about were the little things that had started to annoy me. Habits that other people might find endearing were driving me insane, like the way he kept going on about *Table for Two*'s grosses as it opened in more territories. Or how he kept swapping scar stories with Liz while I was trying to eat lunch.

But it was the new habit that had started when he'd said good night to me after dinner with my parents that was really getting on my nerves. It had been almost a full week and I still hadn't found a way to politely tell him to knock it off.

"Hi, honeybunch," Connor said as he

leaned in for a kiss when he met me in the commissary for lunch on Friday.

I tried not to cringe at the lame nickname. Call it a personal quirk, but I'm not a fan of terms like "honey" or "sugar" or "sweetie" or anything else that implies I could give a person cavities solely from them looking at me.

One glance at the cast on his arm, which was leaning on the table in front of me, and I bit my tongue. I'd gotten myself into this relationship. It was my job to see it through to where it led us. At least until the cast came off in three weeks, four days, two hours, and twenty-five minutes. I would have started at UCLA by then. Maybe our college schedules would determine whether or not the relationship would continue.

"How's the chicken today?" he asked, looking down at my plate.

"Rubbery and dry," I said.

"Just the way I like it," he said. "Back in a sec."

I didn't bother to watch him as he walked to the serving area. I was familiar with the view, nice as it was. The thing was, he had to know something was off.

He was a fairly insightful guy. I couldn't imagine that he was so desperate for a relationship that he'd stay with me just because I seemed more exciting than I really was. He could have almost any girl he wanted. I couldn't be the only one willing to inflict bodily harm.

"So, my saccharine confectionary treat," Liz said from across the table once he was gone. "We've been through another week. Feel any sparks of romance yet?"

"Nothing," I said with a sigh. "Maybe it *is* me."

Liz threw her hand to her forehead. "Perish the thought."

"No, seriously," I said, ignoring her joke at my expense. "I'm messed up."

"Aren't we all?" Liz retorted. Then she got all serious. "Tracy. It's time. Actually, it's past time."

I knew she was right. But that didn't make the situation any easier. My lunch stared up at me, half-eaten. This whole thing made me lose my appetite. "I've got to get out of here," I said, picking up my tour jacket and my tray.

"Hiding from him is not the answer," Liz said.

"I'm not hiding," I said. "I'm thinking. I'll catch up with you later. Meet me in the break room after my tour."

"What do you want me to tell Connor when he gets back?"

"Tell him I had a tour emergency," I said as I hurried to throw out what was left of my lunch and get out of there before he saw me, which would only lead to an awkward conversation.

I wasn't exactly sure what a tour emergency was, but I had faith that Liz would come up with something. I needed some time to figure things out, so I wandered the lot for a while before my afternoon tour.

The walk didn't help me come up with any easy way to end things with Connor, though. I didn't have much practice breaking up with guys I'd been on more than one date with. The few relationships I did have in school were always short and kind of fizzled out on their own. Movie breakups were always hard too. I wasn't sure that going with the experts was a good idea in this case. Look at what happened with Jennifer Aniston and Vince Vaughn. And that was a movie! Oh, wait, I guess it was real life, too.

Considering how well Operation Ro Com had worked—and it had worked for the most part, it just ended badly for Connor and his hand—I thought I might be on my own for this one, unless I could come up with the perfect film example to guide me. I searched my memory for scenes of any good movie breakups, but nothing came to mind short of developing some fatal ailment and having a really tragic good-bye scene. But considering how that option ended in my death, I didn't see it as being viable. And that was the best idea I'd come up with before the lunch hour was up and I had to get back to work.

My Bric-a-brac Shack probation had ended at the beginning of the week, so I was back on tour duty. I even had VIP tours, which meant two hours driving around on the cart. Being able to ride around wasn't as exciting since the weather had been wonderful lately—breezy and cool, which was bizarre for August—but no one was complaining about it.

I met my VIP tour group at the store and loaded them onto the tour cart while the walking-tour people looked on in envy. It was the same every day. The regular tour groups stood there wondering what extra goodies the VIPs would get to see and do since they'd paid twice the price. Would they have a personal sit-down with a real live celebrity? Special access to off-limits sets? A pitch meeting with a movie producer?

Nope. They didn't even get a free gift with purchase.

They did get to ride around in the cart for the two hours, though. And it was a much smaller group. General tour tickets were sold to as many people that walked up to the front gates who wanted to pay the price. The VIP cart only fit eight people, so that made it a much more intimate tour. Seeing as how the store had only managed to fill four of the seats, I was glad to see that it was going to be an even smaller group than usual. I quickly took off and drove around the corner so no last-minute stragglers could join on.

Once the Bric-a-brac Shack was out of sight, I pulled over and listed the tour rules as I had done so many times before: Turn cell phones off; Please don't accost the celebrities if we see any; and No cameras except for designated photo stops.

I had a feeling that this was not going to

be one of my better tours. Aside from my mind being focused on Connor, my heart wasn't in it either. Not to mention that the two couples were from France and only one of the women spoke somewhat passable English. Once she translated the rules, we took off again and started on our way.

Early on, I could tell I was right about the tour. It was one of the slower days on the lot, in spite of the pleasant weather. Everything seemed to be shut down for one reason or another. Then again, it wasn't helpful that three-fourths of my tourists didn't speak a word of English. I can't imagine our ride was exciting for them at all. They were probably expecting something like at Universal Studios where King Kong attacks the tour tram and you get to experience a simulated earthquake. All they got was me speaking in translatable spurts.

"Over here we have the admin building," I said with a wave to my right as I stopped in the designated cart rest spot. "That would be the 'administration' building, I mean. It's where the offices of the studio executives are located." Wait for translation. "You'll notice that the design of the building doesn't match the one beside it." Wait for translation. "That's because every building on the lot is designed to be used for filming." Wait for translation.

But the translation never came.

I looked to the woman who'd been helping me out. "Is there a word you don't understand?"

She didn't respond. She just stared at me like I had sprouted a second head.

Actually, no. That wasn't quite right. She wasn't staring at me. She and her friends were all staring at a point about one foot to my right and a slight bit behind me.

I slowly turned in the direction of their gazes and jumped when I saw Christy Caldwell looking over my shoulder. "Oh!"

"Sorry to scare you there," Christy said with a gentle laugh.

"No problem," I said, looking back to my group. Suddenly, my boring tour had become the highlight of their vacation in Los Angeles. Most of them may not have spoken a word of English, but Christy Caldwell's celebrity status broke any language barrier.

I wanted to give them all kudos for following my rules so well, too. They were doing a great job sitting there, gaping at her. They weren't snapping pictures or accosting the celebrity as they had been firmly instructed not to do.

Actually, I think some of them were paralyzed with excitement. Considering that *Table for Two* was still breaking worldwide box office records, we were all in the presence of the biggest movie star of the moment. Even I was kind of excited, and I'd already spent a whole evening with her before. (Like that made me part of her inner circle, or whatever.)

"I know this is going to get old," Christy said, "but I need a place to hide."

"Again?"

"Long story," Christy said with a glance back to the admin building. "But we gotta move. I saw you passing by from the window of the president's office. My entourage thinks I went to the bathroom. It won't be long before they send out a search party once they realize their meal ticket is MIA."

"Too late," I said as a half dozen executives in suits that cost as much as the dress I'd "borrowed" came spilling out of the building.

Christy hopped in the seat beside me. "Drive!"

I weighed my options in the split second

that followed. There was no way I was getting out of this without being fired. Disappearing on the night of a premiere was one thing. Fleeing from studio executives in a tour cart, with tourists, was quite another.

Then again, it was only a few weeks until school started and I'd be leaving the job, anyway.

I put the cart in drive and floored it before the executives could reach us. "Hang on!"

I heard the French woman yell something that sounded like "Crochet!" but I didn't think anyone back there was taking up knitting. I wished that the tour carts were equipped with seatbelts as I pushed the pedal to the floor and flew alongside the paseo at fifteen miles per hour.

Okay, it wasn't exactly a hugely dramatic exit, but we were going faster than I'd ever gone in a tour cart before.

I hurried us past the admin building, not bothering to pause for Photo Stop #1. I checked in the rearview mirror to see if the executives were still chasing us, and saw that they'd given up the foot race.

I was pretty sure somebody was already calling Carl to tell him I'd "kidnapped"

Christy. Then an APB would go out across the studio. Hopefully, Officer Perkins wasn't on duty during the day.

Sovereign Studios was pretty big, but there was no way a VIP tour cart carrying one blockbuster movie star, four French tourists, and one out-of-her-depth tour guide was going to go unnoticed for long. I needed to find a place to hide until I figured out what the heck was going on. I was about to ask Christy what, exactly, we were running from when I heard the screeching tires behind me.

"They're coming!" Christy shouted. I think the excitement was getting to her. I was sitting right next to her, after all. "Floor it!"

"This *is* floored!" I shouted back. A peek in the rearview showed an electric cart carrying a trio of executives right on our tail. There was *no way* I was getting out of this with my job intact.

The tourists, meanwhile, were laughing and cheering and chattering in French the whole way. I was so glad that I had taken Spanish in school, because I'm not sure I wanted to know what they were saying.

I felt the cart lean to the right as we took a tight turn around the sound-scoring stage.

The cart behind us made the turn without missing a beat. Never in my wildest dreams did I ever imagine I'd one day have a slow-speed chase around Sovereign Studios with America's (latest) Sweetheart beside me. All we needed was a helicopter with a huge spotlight above us and we'd have a great shot for the nightly news.

I zoomed through the New York back-lot, right past Ric's walking tour. The envy those tourists had shown before was nothing compared to their expressions when they saw that a cart chase was part of the VIP tour. And the look on Ric's face was just as priceless.

We escaped from New York like we were being chased by the Transformers. If only my tour cart could've changed into a jet plane.

"They're catching up," Christy said.

I looked in the rearview mirror and saw that Christy was right. The cart was gaining on us. It was a smaller, four-seater model, and I was stuck with the three-row tour version. We also had twice the number of people in our cart. It wasn't like I could drop the tourists off at the next corner and leave them to their own devices.

I swerved to avoid a speed bump and

made a wide turn around a row of trailers. As I turned, I saw that the driver chasing us had taken the bump at full speed, nearly throwing an executive from the cart. The poor guy was hanging off the side by one arm.

"Oooh," Christy said. "That's not good."

Understatement of the decade, I thought.

"They're stopping," Christy said as we drove past the trailers and out of sight. "We could probably move faster on foot," she said.

"Probably," I said. I had to figure out a place to hide before Christy started jettisoning the tourists to lighten our load. Considering I was sure my boss was involved by now, I had to go someplace he'd never think to look for me.

The idea came to me a moment later, and I checked my watch to confirm that we were in time to make it happen. We even had a few minutes to spare. "Anybody want to go to a movie?" I asked.

The French woman translated for her friends, while I hoped they understood it was a rhetorical question. I made another turn as I headed for the backlot screening rooms at a much safer rate of speed, hoping that no one would spot us on the way.

"This movie doesn't star me, does it?" Christy asked.

"I think you have a small cameo," I replied. "It's a clip show."

"Just so long as it's not the Christy Caldwell life story or anything," she said.

"Yeah," I agreed, lightly. "I've already lived enough of that."

We both shared a laugh as we headed to the back end of the studio where the small screening rooms are located, so producers can watch the dailies of the films they're shooting. It's also where they run a twenty-minute presentation on the history of Sovereign Studios that is an optional part of the tour.

The movie was a good way to fill time when there was nothing going on around the studio or it was too hot to be walking for two hours straight. Carl knew I never took tours there. As far as I was concerned, the tourists didn't pay for something they could watch on the classic movie channel. They wanted a Hollywood experience. Well, this particular tour group had already gotten more of a Hollywood experience than any other I'd led, so I figured it was okay to take them there to hide.

"You do find the best parking spots," Christy said as I pulled the cart up behind another big green Dumpster that blocked us from the main road.

I guided everyone to the screening room in time for the film to start. The unseasonably cool August weather had kept the other tour guides on their tours, so we had the place to ourselves. I sat my tourists in the front row and waved to the projectionist to go ahead. Once the lights were out, I joined my new celebrity friend in the back row, where I knew we were safe for at least twenty minutes.

"What are you hiding from today?" I whispered as the film began. "You've got like the highest grossing romantic comedy of all time. I'd think people would lay off for a while and let you bask in the success."

"You're kidding, right?" Christy asked. "Today's meeting is all about the studio, my agent, my manager, and assorted other people—who may or may not work for me—all trying to convince me to sign on for the sequel to *Table for Two*. You'll never guess what they're calling it."

"*Table for Three?*"

"You got it," she said. "Me and my new

beau settle down to raise a family. They've already got the script ready to go into production. Don't these people know that nothing interesting happens beyond Happily Ever After?"

"Tell me about it," I said.

"Trouble in the tour world?" Christy asked.

For reasons I didn't entirely understand, I decided to open up to Christy all about Connor, my scheme, and my fears that I was cold and empty inside when it came to love. I set up the perfect movie plot, found the perfect leading man, and didn't get my happy ending. And the only thing that seemed not to work in the whole Operation Ro Com plan was . . . *me*.

She listened the entire time without interrupting, which more than proved to me that she wasn't a self-obsessed starlet. Considering some of the stories I'd heard about celebrity ego trips, I couldn't imagine many other actors actually letting me babble for more than a minute before turning the conversation back around to themselves.

"Wow," Christy said after I'd unloaded everything. "You totally misunderstood my entire rant about romantic comedies on the night of the premiere."

"No, I got it," I said. "They can be one dimensional and formulaic. *But*, there has to be some level of truth to them for the audience to connect with the emotion. I built my plan off that."

"And you thought that was a good idea?"

"It worked to a point," I said. "But now I'm stuck. I have no idea what to do with Connor."

Christy considered my problem. Several times, she looked like she was going to say something, but stopped herself. Eventually she got an excited look in her eyes and leaned toward me. "Since you like movies so much, let's go back to them for advice. I just read this script for a gritty independent film that I'm pushing to do instead of *Table for Three*. You should do exactly what the heroine in the film does at the end of the movie."

"Yes?" I asked, leaning closer. Christy may have been only a couple of years older than me, but she was a jet-setting movie star. I was sure she knew a thing or two about relationships.

"Exactly," Christy said in a conspiratorial whisper. "This Connor guy. You take him someplace quiet and secluded. You look him in the eyes. And you tell him the truth about how you feel and break up with him."

"That's it?"

"Well, you could always go with the action movie script I read the other day, and fill him with a dozen bullet wounds, leaving him a dead and bloody mess, but I wouldn't recommend it."

"The truth, huh?" I said. It was so simple. So unoriginal. "No games?"

"It's been known to work," Christy said. "Just not in Hollywood. But you might start a trend."

"But that doesn't help me with my love life," I said. "In fact, that's the exact opposite of a love life."

"Well, maybe if you stop playing games, you'll find that love you're looking for," she said. "Look, I've done enough of these movies to know that love doesn't come when you force it. It's not big romantic gestures, or montages, or huge climactic endings. It's the little things. The everyday stuff that no one would pay twelve bucks to see. Like a guy who remembers your favorite kind of ice cream. Or knows when you want to be alone."

"Or makes sure you wear a shawl so you're not cold?" I suggested, as another leading man popped into my mind.

"Exactly," Christy said. "All you have to do is find someone who you're comfortable with. The rest will go from there."

Eighteen

Once the short film was over, we hung back in the screening room for a few minutes so the tourists could take pictures with Christy (even though it wasn't an official tour photo stop). We let the projectionist get in a couple of shots too so he wouldn't rat us out to the studio if it ever came to that. We ran into a bit of a language barrier when the projectionist told everyone to say "Cheese!" and the translator translated it into "Fromage!" They had to redo the picture because the tourists all had their mouths open like they were catching flies.

My new French friends were nice enough to take a shot of Christy and me that they promised to e-mail me when they got home. They also promised to send one to Christy, but were disappointed when she said she didn't give out her e-mail address.

Christy continued along with us on the tour as we finished out the second hour. We figured her people had probably stopped looking by then. Even if they hadn't, she and I had really gotten past the point of caring. I had way more important things on my mind, anyway.

As the tour wrapped up, I drove in the direction of the Bric-a-brac Shack, stopping at the awards case for one last official photo opportunity.

While the tourists were all getting shots of the awards case, I pulled Christy to the side. "They're going to be waiting for us at the studio store when I bring my tour back."

"Then I should go so that you can play innocent," she said. "I think my people probably get the point by now."

"It was great hanging out with you again," I said.

"You too," she said giving me a hug and then slipping a piece of paper into my hand. "Drop me a line if you do get in trouble and I'll straighten things out. Or if you just feel like hanging out."

"I thought you didn't give this out," I said when I saw what it was—a business card with nothing but an e-mail address on it.

"I share it with friends," she said. It was so cool that she thought of me that way. "Just not random travelers."

Christy ditched around the corner before anyone noticed she was gone. It was good, too, because if she had stayed around for formal good-byes, they could have taken forever. I passed along her good-byes to my group, via their translator, and took them back to the studio store where Carl and several agitated people in suits were waiting for me.

I gave them all my best innocent act when I said that I hadn't seen Christy Caldwell since that night at the premiere. I didn't think Carl was buying it, until everyone on my tour backed me up by saying they didn't know what he was talking about. Since three of the four tourists were saying it in French, I think it was the general confusion that got me off the hook.

Because no one thought to check the tourists' cameras for photo evidence, we all got out of there without incident, and I knew I'd be able to finish out my remaining weeks at the studio in peace. I even made twenty bucks in tips.

I left the studio store with my mind made up. I had to be honest with Connor about my feelings and tell him that while I liked him, I simply didn't love him. It couldn't wait another minute. I would go to his office, ask him to go on a coffee break with me, and tell him the truth.

After I changed out of my tour uniform. . . . There was no way I could break up with a guy while dressed in ugly polyester.

The beautiful afternoon seemed all that much nicer once I'd made up my mind about Connor. I wasn't being fair to him, stringing him along. And I didn't need some grand scheme to end it with him. I had to be honest and listen to whatever he had to say to me about the way I'd behaved.

Even with the prospect of facing an ugly reaction ahead of me, I was pretty jazzed about what I was going to do. My mood was considerably lighter now that I had made my decision, and the entire day seemed brighter. With a spring in my step, I walked past the tour office and opened the door to the break room. . . . And froze when I saw a jaw-dropping sight.

I mean, literal jaw-dropping. Like I had just said "Fromage!"

My best friend and my boyfriend had their arms around each other and their lips millimeters from kissing.

At first, I thought I was being *Punk'd*. That they were trying to give me a dose of my own medicine. But when I saw the look of horror on Liz's face, I knew it was real.

I was surprised by the anger that welled up in me. The hurt. The betrayal. I turned away from them and hurried out of the break room and the building—taking care to look both ways as I crossed the street.

"Trace!" Liz called from behind me.

"Go away!" I shouted. I couldn't believe that my best friend would do that to me. My best friend!

"Wait!" she said as she grabbed my arm. Liz always was faster than me. Must be all that outdoor activity. She managed to catch up pretty quickly.

I spun on her and went on the offensive. "How could you?"

"I'm sorry," she said. "Connor came by to talk to me about you. He wanted to try to understand you better. What he should do—"

"Naturally the only way you could explain it was to show him!" I said. It didn't matter that I was about to break up with him. It didn't matter that Liz knew that I never really loved him. She was my best friend. She wasn't supposed to make a move on my guy until it was formally over. And even then, she was supposed to wait an appropriate amount of time and get my permission first.

"No," she said. "It just . . . it just happened. I shouldn't have . . . and well, technically you walked in before anything actually did, but . . . I shouldn't have. And I'm sorry."

We'd reached the parking lot and were starting to cause a little scene. I pulled her behind a huge SUV that blocked us from the onlookers. "So, you haven't been sneaking around behind my back?" I asked.

Liz looked offended. "Why would you think . . . I may be guilty of a lapse in judgment, but to suggest I would go around—"

"Okay, okay," I said, cutting her off. I wasn't about to apologize for offending her. "How did this all happen?"

"We were talking," Liz explained, much more calmly than she had the first time.

"About you. And . . . he's just so confused. He was saying how he liked you, but he wasn't sure if you felt the same way. But at the same time you kept doing all these big-deal dates, like all-day outings and meeting your parents. And you looked so hurt after he broke his arm. So, we got to talking and one thing led to another and . . ."

"Hey," I said, "I've been there. But, how long have you . . ."

I couldn't finish the question. And Liz was having trouble coming up with the answer.

"Since we compared scars," she finally said. "Any guy that talked about trying to keep up with me, even just joking . . . it was a nice idea."

Going back over the past few weeks in my mind, I realized how Liz seemed to have a much better time with Connor than I ever did. They were never at a loss for anything to talk about. And dating him was making me tired, whereas for her it would be a warm-up to a real adventure.

"Please tell me you're not mad," she said.

"I'm not mad," I said. And I was surprised to discover that I meant it. "I'm not mad at all. You've just made this the easiest breakup I've ever had. But . . . go slow with him. He's going to be heartbroken for a while."

Liz and I actually shared a laugh and then we went back to talk to Connor. The breakup was quick and easy, and not even interesting enough of a scene to make it into the first draft of a screenplay.

Once we were officially over, I decided to give Connor and Liz some time to talk. As I left the break room, Liz stopped me. "Stage five," she said.

I wasn't sure what that meant.

"It's where Dex has been hanging out instead of meeting us for lunch this past week," she said. "Maybe you should talk to him."

"Maybe I should," I said. In the movie soundtrack in my mind, I heard the orchestra strike a sharp chord as the realization hit.

Dex knew everything there was to know about me and he still liked me. He was fun and attractive, and he always put my needs first. He had even created the most romantic night I'd ever known and then handed it over for me to use as my own.

But it was the small stuff that was really special. That we could go to the prom together as friends with no expectations and no pressure. That he would agree to take part in a stupid scheme, no questions asked. That he was there when I needed him, but also there when there was no need at all.

He was exactly who I'd been looking for. Someone who I was comfortable with, who I could easily see being a part of the rest of my life, since he'd already been there so long.

Someone I had treated horribly when I effectively abandoned him after our moment in the break room.

I left the building and hopped back in my tour cart, racing across the lot to Stage 5. Halfway there, I realized that I'd totally forgotten to change out of my wretched uniform. Then again, he'd seen me in much worse. The Britney Spears phase I went through back in middle school was a particular horror that came to mind.

I tried the same door that Connor and I had entered on our date. It was unlocked. As soon as I opened it, I heard Dex's voice echoing in the huge space.

I slipped into the soundstage, careful not to let the door make a sound behind me. Dex looked absolutely adorable in the middle of the empty soundstage, rehearsing the lines for his play. I stopped to listen to him for a moment as he worked through a monologue. He really was a wonderful actor. Particularly considering how well he was doing with truly awful dialogue.

He stopped mid-speech when he saw me. "Hi."

"Hi," I said, keeping my distance. "I thought I was supposed to help you run lines."

He shrugged. "I figured you had a lot going on with your boyfriend and all."

"*Ex*-boyfriend," I corrected.

"Ex-boyfriend?"

"I think he's got more in common with your sister," I said.

Even at a distance I could tell that Dex was trying to hold back a smile. "Sorry to hear that."

I didn't bother to hide my grin. "No you're not."

And then it turned into a cheesy scene from an old movie.

I ran across the soundstage and right up to him, planting the kiss to end all kisses on his lips. At first he was too surprised to react, but then he fell right into it and began to kiss back. It was hot. And passionate. And everything that every other kiss I'd ever had in my life had never been.

Someone should have filmed it, because it was the most romantic kiss that ever took place on that soundstage, if not in all of Hollywood.

Not that a camera could have captured what Dex and I were truly feeling in that kiss—just like Uncle Earl's screenplay couldn't re-create what it was that made my parents fall in love. True emotion can't be portrayed onscreen or written in dialogue, no matter how talented the actor, director, or writer may be. That stuff can only be felt in the heart.

And, boy, was I feeling it in that moment.

"Whoa, bro," I said when we broke apart.

Dex laughed. "If we're going to do that again, you're going to have to stop calling me bro. It's too—"

I stopped him by planting another kiss on those lips.

As we kissed, I realized that Operation Ro Com had, in its own way, been a total success. No, it didn't go the way I had intended, but it still followed the formula. I had made the number one biggest romantic comedy mistake that characters were always making in the movies—the one thing that girls from the beginning of film history have been constantly doing.

In my search for love, I had totally overlooked the fact that the perfect guy was right beside me the entire time.

Epilogue

"This is so crazy!" I said as I looked out the window and saw the mob of people on the sidewalk outside the gates of Sovereign Studios. They were standing ten deep behind the barricades, all craning their heads to get a look at who was pulling up.

"Bizarre to see how the other half lives," Liz agreed.

"But kind of fun, too," Dex said. "I've never been invited to a movie premiere before. It's . . . different."

"Get used to it," I told him. "There are plenty more of these in your future."

"Eh," Connor said. "I doubt the movie's going to open that well. Now if it was some big action blockbuster sequel—" Liz stopped him with a playful jab in the ribs. He still liked to talk about opening weekends, but now he did it just to be annoying since Liz had told him how it could be kind of boring to listen to.

The limousine stopped at the edge of the red carpet and one of the greeters outside opened the door for us to step outside. We sort of paused for a moment since this was new territory for all of us.

"You're the movie star," I said to Dex.

"Please," he said. "I play a hot dog vendor with two lines. That I wouldn't have had if it weren't for you. Get out there."

I smiled and stepped out onto the carpet, to the deafening screams of the crowd and the blinding lights from the flash bulbs. It all died down once everyone realized I was just some nobody. But, for that brief moment, I felt like I had arrived.

The feeling came right back to me when Dex took my hand. I smiled at him and gave his hand a squeeze as Liz and Connor got out of the car. The four of us walked down the red carpet together. It was weird experiencing a premiere from this side of things. I could see the pages watching from the entrance of the Sovereign Theater. They looked exactly like Liz and I did the night we worked our first star-studded event.

It had been a year since I'd met Christy Caldwell at the premiere of *Table for Two*, which in its own roundabout way had led to my first kiss with Dex. He and I were still blissfully together. I wasn't sure if we'd get married someday, like my parents had in college, but he and I were enjoying every moment of our relationship and appreciating the time we had together.

Liz and Connor were, too. They had agreed to take things slowly for about one week after their little whatever-it-was in the page break room. Then they jumped out of an airplane together and became a fully committed couple that never spent a free moment apart. It was the first time Liz had ever had a relationship with a guy who could keep up with her. And now they matched each other scar for scar.

A huge cheer from the fans pulled our attention back to the start of the red carpet. The real star of the evening had arrived. Christy Caldwell was stepping out of a limo, along with her latest guy of the moment. She waved to the fans and the cameras, then ditched the guy and the press and ran right up to me when she saw I was there.

"You made it!" Christy said, bouncing up and down on the balls of her feet. I bounced right along with her. Like my being there was a surprise. When I'd received the invitation to the *Table for Three* premiere, I'd called her up and told her I wouldn't miss it for the world. How could I not attend the premiere for the sequel to the film that led to me finally getting the relationship I'd been waiting for?

"I feel like I was in on the deal," I said.

"Hey, you were more useful that day than my agent, my manager, or all those other people that follow me around," she said. "And you're going to be at the opening of my indie film this fall, right?"

"Wouldn't miss it," I said as the cheers around us got louder. After she'd crashed my tour that day, Christy had gone back to her big meeting and insisted that she would only do the *Table for Two* sequel if the studio picked up the distribution on that gritty independent film she had told me about and signed her to do both of them. The Sovereign Studios execs were no dummies when it came to making money, so they agreed right then and there.

"I've got to get back to my people," she said. "I'll see you inside."

"Will you?" I asked, looking toward the poor unsuspecting pages.

"Yes," she said with a laugh. "Well . . . maybe."

I watched her run back to the press line and work the crowd like a pro. For a brief moment, the excitement of the premiere made me want to switch my major to screenwriting. I could write my story of getting together with Dex so I could sell it to the studio, have them hire Christy to star in the film, and we could all have our own big premiere.

But I enjoyed my new major too much to switch again. Film Studies was so right for me. I loved learning all about how a film is made; considering the theory and criticism, putting a movie in a historical context, tracking trends and—yes—even box office numbers. Maybe I could use what I was learning to become a development executive some day. Development execs still get to go to premieres.

Besides, the excitement of attending premieres doesn't go on forever. For me, it was hardly lasting the length of the red carpet. The sights and the sounds were amazing, but if that was all there was in life, it would be kind of empty. None of it really mattered to me anyway, because I had found my happy ending and that was enough.

All the noise and the crowds and the flash bulbs disappeared as Dex and I shared another epic kiss.

About the Author

Before becoming an author, P.J. Ruditis was a tour guide at a major motion picture and TV studio in Hollywood. A highlight of the job was meeting Alicia Silverstone at the premiere of *Clueless*. They didn't hang out together on the roof of a building, but the actress did say "Hi," which was almost as good. Visit P.J. and other Ro Com authors at www .simonpulseromanticcomedies.blogspot.com.

LOL at this sneak peek of

Something Borrowed
By Catherine Hapka

A new Romantic Comedy from Simon Pulse

I hate pink.

Pink is the color of chewed-up bubble gum. Of scar tissue. Of Pepto-Bismol. Totally gagworthy.

Not to mention that it totally clashes with my skin tone and somehow makes my strawberry-blond hair, which I usually love, look bright orange. As a bonus, it also brings out the mud in my hazel eyes.

"It's really not that bad, Ava," my best friend, Teresa, said. She sounded neither convinced nor convincing. In fact, I was pretty sure she'd been averting her eyes ever since I'd wriggled into the Pink Monstrosity.

I was standing in front of the mirror at Olde Main Line Bridal, staring at the baby-butt-pink, puffy-skirted satin blob my older sister, Camille, was inflicting on me for her wedding. I was Camille's maid of honor, probably due to two key facts: (1) I'm her only sister, and (2) most of her friends realized she'd drive them crazy within seconds of launching Operation Perfect Wedding. Having lived with Camille for all of my seventeen and three-quarters years, I was completely aware of both facts. I'd also figured it was pretty much a given that Camille, who was always a bit on the needy side, would morph into the Bridezilla to end all Bridezillas.

However, the pink thing had taken me by surprise. After all, Camille had known *me* for those seventeen-plus years too. You'd think in all that time she would have noticed that while pink worked just fine on her, with her blond hair and blue eyes, it was a Hindenburg-level disaster on me.

Then again, maybe I shouldn't have been surprised by Camille's complete lack of taste, considering that she had chosen Boring Bob as her husband-to-be. In fact, she had dated Bob and only Bob since the dawn of time, aka middle school. Even back then, though I was just eight years old myself, I'd been thoroughly unimpressed. The thirteen-year-old Bob had been one of those kids who got out of gym a lot because of his asthma and paid a more musically hip kid to make a cool mix CD for him to give to Camille on Valentine's Day. Now, some ten years later, Bob had grown up into a total suburban metrosexual, too busy perfecting his hair-gel technique in front of the mirror to actually go out and do anything. Well, unless you counted pasta at the Olive Garden as doing something. Which I certainly didn't.

Anyway, I didn't see the appeal. But I wouldn't expect Clueless Camille to understand. Despite being sisters, the two of us had never had much in common.

I twirled in front of the mirror, trying to convince myself that Teresa was right and the dress wasn't that bad. On the plus side, it did make me look much more hourglassy than I really was, thanks to the enormous pouffy sleeves and bubble-butt skirt. Maybe my cute face and outgoing personality would be enough to pull off the look. . . .

But no. The Pink Horror was just too strong. It was even starting to overcome my natural sense of optimism and *joie de vivre*.

"Did I ever mention that I hate pink?" I mumbled with a defeated sigh.

Teresa got up and came over to stand next to me. Her reflection in the mirror looked refreshingly nonpink. Her thick dark hair was pulled back from her gorgeous-without-a-speck-of-makeup (not even concealer—talk about unfair!) high-cheekboned face. She was wearing denim cut-offs and a white fitted T-shirt with the faintest hint of faded green horse slobber on the sleeve. Even though I was standing on that little platform they always have in bridal shops, Teresa was still a bit taller than I was.

"Look, Ava," she said in her best listen-up voice. She'd developed it over her years of dealing with horses, and it worked pretty well on people, too. "Unless you decide to run away from home in the next two weeks, you're going to have to show up at that wedding in this dress. So you might as well suck it up and deal."

That was just like Teresa. Despite her sultry foreign-film-star looks, she was definitely the no-nonsense, pragmatic type. I'd always appreciated that about her, especially since I tended toward the happy-go-lucky and giddily impractical myself. Or so Teresa had always told me. And she was almost always right.

That didn't mean I always had to admit it. "You're just saying that because you won't have to witness my fashion catastrophe in person," I pointed out. "I still don't know how you managed to make that happen."

She smiled serenely. "Don't be silly. I signed up for that internship way before I found out Camille's wedding date."

"Whatever. You're just going to have to deal with the fact that you're missing the social event of the season. People from Ardmore to Malvern are going to be talking about this wedding for eons, and you're going to miss it just for the chance to help a bunch of foreign horses improve their sex lives."

Teresa kept smiling. She didn't seem too broken up about the idea of missing the wedding. In less than two weeks she would be leaving for a monthlong internship on a horse-breeding farm in Germany. I'd been kind of bummed when I'd first heard about the trip. Teresa was a year older than I was and had just finished her first year at the University of Pennsylvania. Even though Penn was just a few miles up the road in Philadelphia, it had been a big change to go from seeing her every day to only on the occasional weekend. I'd imagined us making up for lost time over the summer: lots of days hanging out together by my family's pool, at her barn, at the mall; lots of evenings double-dating with our respective boyfriends.

Not that I'd been particularly looking forward to spending more time with Teresa's boyfriend. Teresa and Jason had met at a college party, and I'd disapproved practically from the moment I met him six months ago. I still had no idea what she saw in him. I mean, sure, he was cute. Very cute, as a matter of fact: tall, sort of tousley brown hair, great butt. Plus he was smart, with a killer smile and a quick wit. For a second when I first met him, I'd been almost envious.

Almost. See, it hadn't taken me long to realize that despite those surface charms, Jason was almost as Boring Bob–like as Bob himself, what with the perfect hair and the perfectly preppy clothes and that smug little smirk of his that always made me suspect he was secretly laughing at me. I wasn't sure of his feelings toward the Olive Garden, but then again I wasn't sure about his feelings about much of anything. He barely talked about himself at all and seemed to have no particular interests other than watching basketball on TV and messing around with his computer. Like I said, boring.

Despite all that, I'd been more than

willing to tolerate his dullness if it meant spending more time with Teresa this summer. Of course, now we had a month less than I'd planned thanks to that internship. When I realized she would be hopping the plane for Munich exactly one day before Camille's Big Day, my wistful disappointment changed to sheer envy. Unfortunately, it was far too late by then to sign up for that internship myself—not to mention the fact that horses made me a little nervous, and they mostly seemed to feel the same way about me.

The bridal-shop woman had been busy on the phone for the past few minutes. But now she came bustling over to check on us. She was one of those quintessential Main Line ladies of a certain age: carefully frosted and coiffed hair courtesy of Toppers Spa or some such place, clothes so conservative that you just knew they had to be expensive, and a touch of plastic surgery to pull it all together.

"How are we doing over here, ladies?" she asked in what I could only describe as a brisk coo. "Miss Hamilton, the gown looks fabulous! Though I think we may need to take it in a smidge more at the bust. . . ."

She pulled a tape measure out of her pocket and went to work.

I fought the urge to roll my eyes at Teresa. If there's one thing even more fun than trying on a fugly pink dress, it's standing there with a complete stranger poking at your chest while basically telling you you have no boobs. Isn't that exactly how any girl would love to spend a gorgeous summer Sunday afternoon?

"Hey, Ava, I think I hear your phone ringing." Teresa glanced in the direction of the dressing room. "Want me to grab it?"

"No, thanks," I said. "Let it go to voice mail. It's probably just Mom again, complaining about Camzilla's latest breakdown."

Teresa grinned. "Right. What was it last time? Problems with the cake?"

"Keep up; that was last week. Today it was something about canapés, I think. Mom didn't go into detail in her message, but I'm pretty sure it involved the end of life as we know it."

The bridal-shop lady glanced at us both with a sort of *tut-tut* look on her face, though she was far too well-bred to say anything. Or maybe it was because she'd met my sister and realized what we were dealing with.

It seemed like forever before the bridal lady was satisfied that, yes, the Pink Thing could be properly molded to my B-minus boobage. Finally, she stepped back and tucked away her tape measure.

"All right, Miss Hamilton," she said, "we'll be sure to have your dress ready to try on again by the next fitting."

"What if it still doesn't fit right?" I asked with a sudden burst of hope. "The wedding is two weeks from yesterday. Is there any chance it might not be ready?"

Her reassuring smile made my new-found hope fizzle out. "Our most talented seamstress will be working on it. It will fit; don't worry. Just leave it on the hook in the dressing room, and we'll see you again on Thursday for the final fitting."

"Come on, Ave. Let's go get you changed and get out of here." Teresa grabbed my hand and dragged me off the little platform. We pushed our way past a rack of plastic-shrouded bridal white and through an arched doorway into the dressing room.

In the same way that "dress" means

something completely different in Bridal Shop Land, so does "dressing room." Instead of the toilet-stall-like individual enclosures you usually find at the mall, this place had just one big, open room, complete with framed wedding photos on the walls, several tasteful white upholstered sofas and chairs scattered around, and a couple of those little platforms with accompanying three-way mirrors. The day Camille tried on her gown for the first time, there had actually been another bride, her mother, and about half a dozen giggling friends in there with us. I'd expected Camille to blow her top at that, but she'd been so busy freaking out over how the (pure white) buttons didn't *exactly* match the color of the (pure white) fabric that I'm not sure she even noticed.

Today Teresa and I had the place to ourselves, and I was glad about that. The fewer witnesses to my pink shame the better. I'd dropped my clothes on one of the white tufted chairs, and they were right there waiting for me, although apparently Bridal Lady had sneaked in and folded them while we were outside. Folded or not, I'd never been so glad to see them.

Unfortunately, as I mentioned, the deluxe

dressing room also included a couple of those giant three-way mirrors. That meant I was subjected once again to the view of myself encased in the Pink Horror.

"This is really going to happen, isn't it?" I asked Teresa as I stared at my cotton-candy-colored reflection. "I'm actually going to have to wear this thing in public."

"*And* be memorialized forever in the wedding photos," Teresa said. Apparently realizing it wasn't the most tactful comment in the world, she reached over and squeezed my arm. "But don't worry. If anyone can pull off the look, you can. Besides, you'll probably forget you're wearing it once the reception starts and you're dancing the night away with Lance."

"That's true." I brightened a bit at the thought. Lance and I had been together for nearly three months. As Teresa would say, that was practically a record for me, Ms. Short Attention Span. But Lance was pretty special. For one thing, he was superhot, with this spiky white-blond hair and biceps that would make Michelangelo drool. But it wasn't his looks that made me really fall for him. And it certainly wasn't the fact that he was Boring Bob's stepcousin. No, the first thing I adored about Lance was his incredible passion for cars.

Not that I was any kind of gearhead myself. I didn't even have a car of my own—my parents always said that if I wanted one, I could pay for it myself, and somehow I'd always found better things to do with the paycheck from my part-time job than spend it on boring stuff like insurance and gas. Besides, why go to all that trouble? I had enough friends with cars that I could almost always get a ride. And in a pinch my parents would usually let me borrow one of theirs as long as I promised to top off the tank.

In any case, even if my own motor didn't race at the very sight of a perfectly restored '65 T-bird, I could appreciate that kind of passion in Lance. I liked guys who had strong interests, who went out and *did* things. Okay, so after about the fourth time, those impromptu drag races weren't that exciting anymore. And maybe spending at least half our dates listening to Lance talk about rotors and spark plugs was getting a *teensy* bit dull. But even so, after almost three whole months, I was still smitten. Or at least interested enough to stick with Lance for a while—definitely through the wedding, for sure. After that, we would just have to see.

For now the important thing was that he was almost as crazy about me as he was about cars. And that he'd look awesome in a tux as long as he got the axle grease out from under his fingernails. That reminded me—I really needed to talk to him about the fingernail thing. . . .

"Turn around," Teresa ordered. "I'll get your zipper."

"Don't forget the stupid little pearl buttons at the top," I reminded her as I turned my back. "Camille had them special-ordered from, like, Zimbabwe or somewhere. If we lose any, she'll freak."

"How will we be able to tell?" Teresa joked. Her graceful fingers made short work of the pearl buttons and the zipper. "There you go. Free at last."

Well, not quite. See, the Pink Blob was designed in such a way that it was almost impossible to shimmy it off over my hips and butt, despite the fact that I'm not exactly J. Lo in that department. That meant it had to go off the same way it had gone on: over my head.

"A little help here?" I said to Teresa. "And

no comments about the SpongeBobs this time, please."

Teresa grinned but stayed quiet as she stepped forward. I just happened to be wearing a pair of garish and slightly baggy SpongeBob SquarePants panties that day. That was what happened when you let yourself get behind on laundry because you were so busy bridesitting. Still, it was one more reason I was really glad we were alone in the dressing room this time.

The Pink Horror was halfway over my head, stuck somewhere around my shoulders and completely blocking my vision, when I heard footsteps approaching from nearby. I froze, picturing Ms. Tastefully Coiffed Bridal Shop Lady walking in with a bride or two in tow and fainting dead away at the sight of my bright yellow panties.

But what I heard next was far more horrible than anything I could have imagined. "Hey, are you guys almost done in . . ."

I yanked down the dress as fast as I could. I recognized that voice. Sure enough, Teresa's boyfriend was standing in the dressing-room doorway, slack-jawed and staring at me in all my butt-hanging-out, SpongeBob-underpanted glory.

"What are you *doing* in here, Jason?" Teresa exclaimed, horrified. "This is a women's dressing room!"

"Sorry." Jason snapped his mouth shut. We'd left him out in his Prius in the parking lot, reading a book. Since neither Teresa nor I had access to a car that day, she'd sweet-talked him into playing chauffeur. "I—I wasn't expecting—," he stammered. Jason was the type of guy who was rarely at a loss for words. But he was now. Score one for me and SpongeBob. "That is, at the mall the dressing rooms are usually . . ."

Meanwhile, I was frantically trying to cover various body parts with pink satin. This was just my luck. I let my laundry pile up for a day or two and I end up flashing the world with the novelty panties my friends got me as a joke.

"What do you want, anyway?" Teresa asked Jason impatiently.

Jason cleared his throat. From the expression in his greenish-gray eyes, I couldn't quite tell if he was amused or frightened.

"Never mind," he said, shooting one last glance in the direction of my now-mercifully-hidden underpants before turning away. "I'll just, um, wait in the car."

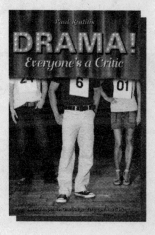

Public Displays
of
Confession

Like a guilty-pleasure celeb magazine,
these juicy Hollywood stories
will suck you right in. . . .

★ ★ ★

Lincoln Township Public Library
2099 W. John Beers Rd.
Stevensville, MI 49127
(269) 429-9574